Y0-BZY-436

Protected

by a

SEAL

HOT SEALS

Cat Johnson

Copyright © 2015 Cat Johnson

All rights reserved.

ISBN-978-1511884211
ISBN-1511884215

CHAPTER ONE

As he raised the beer bottle to his lips, Rick Mann heard it, but he didn't believe it. At least, he didn't *want* to believe it.

The sound invading his peace and quiet was enough to ruin his enjoyment of even his favorite brand of icy cold brew. He lowered the bottle without taking a sip and smothered a cuss.

Nope. That was not the banging of the headboard against the wall of his sister's bedroom. Again. For the second time in as many hours. Definitely. Not.

Rick closed his eyes and did his best to believe his own lie, but it wasn't going to work.

No matter how hard he tried and willed it to be so, the fact remained he was hearing something no brother should be forced to listen to—his best friend in bed with his sister.

It was his own fault, he supposed. Rick did share a house with Darci. And Rick had sent her away on an assignment with his buddy and former SEAL teammate Chris. With his blessing, no less.

But damn, he'd never expected *this* to be the result.

Almost a month after they'd announced they were dating, Darci and Chris were obviously still in the honeymoon period of the relationship.

It was enough to make Rick want to rip his own ears off.

Drawing in a deep breath, he set his jaw and reached for the television remote control.

He mashed the button with his thumb until the sound of the show airing rose enough he could no longer hear the incredibly disturbing and damn rude noise coming from the vicinity of Darci's bedroom.

Couldn't they do this shit while he was at work?

Rick raised the bottle to his lips again and drew in a big swallow. He needed it to dull the horror.

The combination of noise, beer and the History Channel actually worked. Thank God. Rick made it through two commercial breaks without hearing another sound from the bedroom region of the house. Excellent.

"Hey." The sound of Chris's voice behind him had Rick jumping.

Happy inside his bubble of beer and the program commemorating the 90th anniversary of Czar Nicholas II abdicating his throne in the midst of World War I, Rick hadn't heard Darci's door open.

Rick aimed the remote at the television and lowered the volume. "Hey."

Chris frowned. "What's wrong?"

Rick supposed his greeting hadn't sounded all that warm and cozy and Chris had noticed. He scowled. "What could be wrong?"

Chris lifted one shoulder. "I don't know. That's why I asked."

It wasn't worth bringing it up. It's not like Rick's complaining would change anything. These two were like dogs in heat. Rick realized Chris was still standing, waiting for an answer.

At least his friend was dressed. Only in shorts and a tank top but it could have been worse. He hadn't gotten comfortable enough to start walking around the house in his underwear yet. Or worse, naked.

Hoping that day never came. Rick focused on the television. "It's nothing."

Chris moving in front of Rick and directly in front of the screen ruined his plan to lose himself again in the program. It was a widescreen television, but Chris was pretty wide himself.

Arms crossed, legs planted firm, the man obviously wasn't moving.

Rick sighed and relented. "The walls are thin here. Okay?"

Realization must have hit Chris. He closed his eyes for a second. "Oh. Sorry about that. We didn't realize you could hear."

Rick let out a snort. "Oh, I can. Believe me."

"I can ask Darci to come over to my place when you're home."

Perfect. Then Rick could be a real loser, alone in the house instead of just feeling lonely around the happy couple. At least now, he had company when they did emerge from the bedroom.

The solution didn't seem all that much better than the problem.

"Don't worry about it." Rick took another swallow. "You hungry?"

"Starving. Darci and I are fixin' to order something. You in?"

"Yeah, sure. What are you gonna get?"

"Darci wants Indian food. You okay with that?"

Rick shot Chris a look. "She's always trying to get us to order that." And Rick always said no, but apparently she'd gotten one over on Chris. She'd convinced him to get Indian food while she had him in a sex haze.

"So, that's a no then?" Chris looked a little torn. Friend versus girlfriend.

After hearing that bed banging, Rick knew exactly which side Chris would land on the choice of take-out. "No, it's fine. Go ahead. I'll give it a try."

Who knows? Maybe Rick might actually like the shit.

"A'ight." Chris flopped backward into the easy chair.

"Aren't you ordering it?"

"Oh, hell no. Darci's doing it. I wouldn't know what to order anyway. You know what you'd want?"

Rick leveled his gaze on Chris. "What do you think?"

"Yeah, that's what I thought." Chris shook his head. "You'd never know there was once a time we were both eating goat meat and pretending to like it."

"That is exactly why I don't feel the need to try any of this weird shit now."

"It's not weird." Darci's voice came from down the hall before she appeared in the living room. "It's good and you two are going to like it and I'm going to say *I told you so* when you do."

Rick craned his head to see her, dressed in her yoga pants and a sweatshirt. "You wish."

She lifted one brow. "We'll see."

"Yes, we will." Rick let out a humph. Chris's soft chuckle caught Rick's attention. "And what're you laughing at?"

"Nothing. Just missing my little brother about now, is all."

"Where is he?" Rick asked.

Chris cocked a brow and didn't answer and Rick remembered the important detail he'd forgotten. That Brody was still active duty in the teams. Actually, that fact was easy to remember. It was that Rick no longer was, and therefore no longer had security clearance, that he'd like to forget.

He scowled. "Never mind. Forget I asked."

Rick and Chris were both retired now and technically civilians so chances were good that Chris wouldn't know where his brother was anyway. And if he did know, he wouldn't repeat it with Darci around.

Besides her being a civilian, if his sister ever knew half of the shit he'd done in the teams she'd freak the hell out. Rick didn't need that kind of drama.

Chris didn't either now that he was dating Darci.

Of course, after what Chris had subjected Rick to today, maybe he deserved a little torture as payback.

Darci came back from the kitchen, phone in

hand. "The restaurant won't deliver this far. I'll have to go pick it up."

Chris planted his two hands on the arms of the chair he'd looked pretty comfortable in before Darci's announcement and hoisted himself to his feet. "I'll drive you."

"You don't have to do that." In a tone Rick recognized well, Darci had said one thing while obviously meaning another.

Rick waited to see if Chris would get caught in the trap.

"Nope. I insist. Just let me throw on my socks and sneakers." Chris hadn't fallen for it, proving he was smarter when it came to women than Rick gave him credit for.

That was for the better anyway. Rick didn't need to listen to them fighting all night. That might be worse than hearing them in bed.

"Okay. Thank you." She smiled sweetly and accepted the kiss Chris pressed to her head on his way past her.

Rick watched the whole thing unfold, not feeling at all guilty that he got to stay home while Chris had to go out. If Chris wanted to be with Darci, then he'd have to do her bidding.

All Rick knew was that he wasn't the one who had to drive her over, and that was good enough for him.

Darci came over and scowled at the television set. "War stuff?"

"Yes. It's educational. More than those shows about the housewives of wherever that you like to watch."

She frowned at him. "You know I haven't watched the Real Housewives since the first season. It went downhill after that."

The show started out so badly, it didn't have all that far to fall, in Rick's opinion. Not in the mood to debate the point, he kept that to himself.

"A'ight. We can head on out as soon as I find the keys to my truck." Brows drawn low, Chris glanced at the kitchen counter. "You see them?"

"Yup, I know where they are. They were in the pocket of your jeans when I was doing laundry. I put them on my dresser in the bedroom." Darci scampered off, down the hall to retrieve Chris's keys, while Rick took that opportunity to shoot Chris a glance.

"She's doing your laundry now?"

Chris lifted one shoulder and grinned. "What can I say? I'm not gonna tell her no."

Rick shook his head at the domestic bliss surrounding him. It was enough to make a man barf.

"You know . . . " Chris began the sentence in a tone Rick recognized well. A lecture was coming and he wasn't sure he wanted to hear it. Unfortunately, there was usually no way to stop the southern ramblings of Chris Cassidy once they began.

Rick sighed and angled himself to face Chris better. "Yes?"

"I know what's eating you."

"Oh, do you? And what's that?" Rick asked, interested to hear the answer.

"You're missing the action."

Rick let out a huff. "You think? You mean you

don't believe sitting in front of a bank of security monitors day and night is stimulating enough for me?"

"Unless there's some terrorists sneaking around that job of yours, looking to blow up the nuclear reactor and half the state with it, no. There's not. It's getting to you. Believe me, I know what it's like to be running on adrenaline and energy drinks one day and sunk into the sofa looking for something that won't make you want to blow your brains out on TV the next."

"There's one big difference though."

"What's that?" Chris asked.

"You chose to retire. Getting out wasn't exactly my choice."

His knee blowing out during a training exercise, the realization that he'd have compromised the safety of the team if it had happened on an op, and the Navy medically retiring him had all led to Rick's current situation.

Chris drew in a breath, clearly about to say something when Darci came back down the hall. "Sorry I took so long. I decided to change clothes quick."

Like the gentleman he always was, Chris turned his full attention away from Rick and on to Darci. "And you look real pretty, darlin'." He took the keys she held out and glanced at Rick. "We'll be back in a few."

As he grabbed Darci's hand to lead the way to the front door, she glanced back. "Get the plates and forks out of the dishwasher? They're all clean."

"Yeah. Okay."

This was his life now. He'd gone from cleansing the world of terrorism, to unloading the clean dishes. His biggest battle nowadays was against his sister for control of the television remote.

Chris was right. Rick missed the action. More than he'd ever imagined.

He had some thinking to do. As he stood and felt the twinge in his left knee, he wondered if that life was even possible for him anymore.

CHAPTER TWO

SIERRA COX

That was the only thing written on the envelope on the dressing table in her trailer on the studio lot.

No stamp. No return address. No address at all. Just her name, written in black marker in big block letters.

Sierra glanced from the large manila envelope to her manager. "Roger, did you put this here?"

"Put what where?" The thirty-something year old blond man, who was pretty enough he should be in front of the camera rather than behind it managing her, looked up from his cell phone.

Roger Herndon would be a real lady killer if his preference didn't run toward the male gender. That still didn't prevent women from throwing themselves at him at every event and party.

"This envelope." She turned away from her dressing table to face Roger head on.

Lifting his eyebrows, Roger shook his head. "Wasn't me. I've never seen that envelope before. Must have been someone else."

"Who?"

He lifted one shoulder. "Any number of people could have dropped it there, I suppose."

Sierra frowned. The idea that any number of people were wandering through her trailer on the movie lot wasn't reassuring. During filming she spent more time here than anywhere else. It was her home away from home.

She didn't welcome any invasion of her privacy at any time, but knowing someone had been in her private domain when she hadn't been there felt even worse. "We need to lock that door whenever I'm not here."

"Amy has to come in to stock your fridge every day."

"We'll give her a key." It wasn't the intern she was worried about. It was that apparently anyone could come and go as they pleased.

"What if there's an updated script the director needs you to look over?" Roger asked.

"Maybe we need to install a mail slot for things like that." She shot him a look that she hoped said victory was hers.

"May I point out that if you had a mail slot, that mysterious envelope that has apparently disturbed you would still be inside your trailer and freaking you out?"

"Yes, but the person who brought it here wouldn't have been."

"Fine. Mail slot aside, there's also staff who

comes in to clean when you're not around. Or did you think fairies emptied your garbage and scrubbed your toilet?"

"Very funny." Sierra wrinkled her nose at him and wondered why she put up with his crap.

Possibly because Roger was the one person in the world she trusted. Even her parents had lost that privilege when they'd mismanaged her finances to a criminal degree when she'd still been a minor.

But part of the reason she trusted Roger was that he wasn't a yes-man. For better or worse, he told her exactly how things stood, whether she liked what she heard or not.

"So, aren't you going to open it?" Roger took a step closer, his eyes focused on the object in question.

There was something about the seemingly innocuous envelope that had her inner voice shouting and put her on edge. "You go ahead if you want."

"All right." His gaze cut to her before he reached for it. He slipped one finger under the adhesive flap.

Watching him, Sierra hissed in a breath. "Be careful. Don't get a paper cut."

"I assure you, I'll survive."

"Go ahead and joke, but I'm serious, Roger. You don't know who that's from or what's inside. It could be—I don't know—anthrax or something."

He paused in his opening, but obviously not because he shared her concern, judging by his snicker. "Why in the world would there be anthrax in here?"

"I don't know. There are lunatics everywhere." There was something making her gut twist and she didn't know why. She only knew that the feeling started when she first saw that envelope on her dressing table.

"Not that I have personal experience, but I don't think anthrax is quite this heavy." He weighed the envelope in his hand. "Most likely, we're good."

He was teasing her, but Sierra still didn't let herself relax. She knew she wouldn't be able to breathe freely again until she saw what was inside.

A wrinkle formed between Roger's brows as he glanced up. He must have finally taken her concern seriously. "You really are worried."

She opened her eyes wider. "Yes. That's what I've been trying to tell you."

"But why?"

"The whole thing is weird. That just appears out of nowhere with nothing but my name written like . . . like . . . "

"Like what?" He looked down at the envelope again.

"Like a ransom note."

He cocked one brow. "I believe ransom notes are usually made from individual letters cut out of magazines. This, as you saw, is hand written."

Sierra let out a huff. "You're right. It's much more like a serial killer would write it than a kidnapper."

Roger rolled his eyes. "You've been watching too many movies. I'm opening it and putting this whole ridiculous discussion to rest. It's probably proofs from last week's photo shoot. Or a copy of that interview you gave Vanity Fair."

She didn't remind him that both of those things would likely come by email, not in a creepy envelope. Crossing her arms, she waited for whatever mysteries hid within the manila to be revealed.

As Roger again slid his finger between the flap and the envelope, she took a single step back. He leveled a glare at her. "Is that extra foot of separation going to save you from the anthrax?"

She pulled her mouth to the side, annoyed with his smart ass comment. "It might."

Roger peeked inside the envelope. As his grin at her expense disappeared the feeling of doom riding her doubled. "What's wrong?"

He pulled out a stack of papers before he glanced up. "Um, it's probably nothing."

The blood draining from his face as he flipped through the pages didn't back up that statement.

"Roger . . ." Sierra took a step forward. "Let me see."

He pressed his lips together and hesitated before he drew in a breath. He held out the stack toward her, still looking reluctant to hand over what the ominous envelope held.

She closed the space between them with a few steps and took the papers, her hand shaking as she did so. Turning them toward her she saw what looked like digital photos printed out on computer paper. One of her out for her daily run. Another of her getting into her car outside the hair salon. She recognized the outfit she was wearing in that photo. It had to be taken just last week when she'd gotten her highlights touched up.

"They could have been taken by paparazzi." At Roger's suggestion, Sierra glanced up.

"How did he get inside to deliver it?" she asked.

"Maybe the envelope was dropped off at the front gate of the lot and one of the crew brought it here."

The paparazzi theory would have made sense except for the next picture Sierra saw in the stack. It was of her inside her hotel room, sitting at the table eating. Heart pounding, she held it up for Roger. "How'd they take this one?"

He looked from the picture to her. "Through your hotel room window with a zoom lens?"

The moment she got to her hotel she was closing the blackout curtains and not opening them again for the duration of her stay.

The thought of spending the night alone in her suite, knowing someone was watching her, was frightening. Maybe she could convince Roger to sleep on the sofa in the living room of the suite. Hell, he could sleep in the bed with her if it meant she didn't have to sleep there alone. Not that she'd get any sleep after this.

The question still remained, more than how the pictures were taken, was why? And why deliver them to her here and now?

Afraid of what else she would find, Sierra warily looked at the next page in the stack.

It was different. There was another photo of her—this time smiling at someone she couldn't see in the frame of the picture—but this one had words scrawled across it in what looked like the same black marker as the envelope.

What she read had her blood running cold.

You can't see me but I can see you.

The room seemed to sway as the darkness crept around the edges of her vision, narrowing her sight to just the dressing table in front of her. Sierra reached out to steady herself, letting the papers scatter onto the surface.

"Sierra." Roger was next to her in a split second, holding her upright with a strength that belied his trim build.

She swallowed hard and struggled to slow her breathing. "I'm all right."

He let out a breath. "No. None of this is all right and I'm going to take care of it right now."

"What can you do?"

"First, get you sitting down before you fall down."

"I'm fine."

"Sit anyway."

The dizziness had passed, which was a miracle considering her pulse rushed so loudly in her ears she could barely hear Roger. But she was shaking and sitting wouldn't be a bad thing. She did as told and eased into the chair.

She glanced up and caught a glimpse of herself in the mirror. The wild-eyed fear she saw was not at all comforting. Sierra turned in the chair to face toward Roger and away from the reflection of the frightened woman who looked nothing like her.

Acting calmer than she felt, she asked, "What do we do?"

He already had his cell phone out. "We hire

security."

The studio lot had security. The hotel had security. Obviously none of that had worked, so Roger must mean something else. More personal. "Like a bodyguard?"

"Exactly."

Her privacy was the thing Sierra valued more than all else. Now she'd have a man dedicated to doing nothing but watching her every move, day and night. But whoever had taken those photos was already doing that.

There were times she hated this business. Enough that she sometimes dreamed what it would be like to quit and go back to being nobody. Anonymous. Able to go shopping, or jogging, or hell, dancing, without having the cameras in her face and her face on the front page of every tabloid.

This situation was more than over eager paparazzi. This was someone scary. Possibly deranged. That was the only reason Sierra nodded her head and said, "Okay. I'll agree to hiring someone."

With the cell pressed to his ear, Roger let out a snort. "Do you really think I was giving you a choice in the matter?"

In spite of it all, she couldn't help her short laugh as Roger turned into a protective mother hen. "No."

Still, the irony wasn't lost on her that to gain back her privacy, she'd have to sacrifice what little of it she had left.

CHAPTER THREE

Even Sun Tzu wasn't enough to keep him entertained.

Rick put down his cell and rubbed his eyes. Reading on his phone's screen wasn't ideal, but he had to do something to occupy his brain.

He was so bored this shift, he was ready to crawl right out of his skin. Rereading one of his all time favorite books seemed like the best way to keep him from blowing up the nuclear reactor where he worked just so he'd have some excitement.

But *The Art of War* wasn't doing it for him today. He had a feeling nothing would as long as he continued to work here. In this action-less pit that sucked out a man's soul, one long eventless hour at a time.

All right. Maybe it wasn't that bad and he should be grateful to have a steady job, but he wasn't feeling very fortunate at the moment.

Chris had been right. Rick missed the action and the camaraderie and yeah, the adrenaline rush.

He'd become an adrenaline junkie being in the teams all those years. All the guys he knew had. He knew going cold turkey when he had been medically retired would be tough, but it had been way harder than he'd ever imagined.

Visually, he swept the bank of black and white security monitors in front of him.

Black and white. Just like his life felt lately when it used to be filled with bursts of color.

Rick let out a sound of derision at his own bullshit.

Too much time spent alone did that to a guy he supposed—made him philosophical, and not in a good way.

The night shifts were the worst, when there was a skeleton crew working. At least during the day shift there was more action to watch on the damn screens.

He needed to look for a new job. But his annual job review was coming up and with it, more vacation days. Days he could use working ops for GAPS.

A new job would mean starting from scratch and having to earn those days off all over again over time. Time he didn't want to wait.

The existence of Guardian Angel Protection Services and the fact he was even a small part of the company his former SEAL teammates had formed might be the only thing keeping him sane.

Nope, until GAPS was up and running at full speed, and had enough work to employ Rick steadily enough he didn't have to hold down another job, the smart move was to stay working where he was.

He just hoped it didn't cost him his sanity.

The text came through right after Rick, in his desperation, had resorted to calculating how many more minutes he had until his shift was over—a hundred and thirty one. Just as he was considering seeing if he could stream a movie on his cell phone's browser, the vibrating buzz of the cell on the desk in front of him had Rick diving to look at the readout.

He'd take any distraction at this point. Even a text from his sister would be welcome. One glance told him this wasn't from Darci. It was a group text to all the guys.

GAPS MEETING 19:30 @JON'S

Rick had to stifle his shout of excitement. A GAPS meeting meant there must be a job on the horizon.

Jon wasn't the type to call them all together just for the sake of meeting. They'd all had enough of that bullshit when they'd been on active duty.

That was one thing that made working with a private military contractor different and better. That was only one reason Rick was happy to be a part of this particular PMC with his friends.

A GAPS job meant there could be some excitement in his near future. That thought alone was enough to have Rick standing up and pacing the room with excess energy.

His body remembered what having a mission felt like and it didn't care there was one hundred and thirty minutes left for him to be cooped up in here.

He'd wait it out. There was nothing else to do. But in the meantime, Rick replied to the group text.

I'M THERE!

As he waited, biding time, the rest of the guys replied too. Chris with a *HELL YEAH*, and Zane with a *DELAYED ETA NLT 20:00*.

Zane would be half an hour late?

He rolled his eyes at that, but honestly Rick didn't care all that much. He'd be there early and chomping at the bit.

The text conversation continued as Jon asked if Brody was back in town. When Chris responded yes, Jon said to bring him along.

That added another element of interest to Rick's boring shift.

What was this job that Jon wanted Brody—still active duty in DEVGRU—there to consult with them?

Rick's agitation and his anticipation to get the night moving ratcheted up another notch.

Damn, he did need action to feel alive.

If he'd needed any more proof, this was it—his pacing back and forth in the security office like a caged tiger desperate to get out. He would have to consider what to do about that reality later.

Right now he was too excited about tonight's meeting to put a damper on it with introspection.

The door of the office swung open and he jumped. Mike walked in and turned to face Rick standing in the far corner of the room with his cell in his hand.

Mike frowned. "Everything all right?"

"Yeah, fine. Just making plans for later after I get off."

A wide grin lit his coworker's face. "Lucky you. Anything good?"

"It could be but I don't want to jinx it until I'm sure."

Mike's disappointment was clear in his sigh and his crestfallen expression. Apparently they both needed some inspiration to get through the workday.

"So, uh, remember when I took those extra shifts for you so you could go on your honeymoon?" Rick asked.

"Yeah. Why? What's up? You need me to cover a shift for you?"

"Well, nothing yet, but if it turns out I need a couple of shifts off, you think you'd be able to cover for me?"

"If I'm not already on, yeah. No problem. Bree and I are saving for a house and I could use the extra hours, so sure."

That was the second best news Rick had gotten all day—the first being the meeting that could very well be the end of his dry spell. An oasis in what was a desert devoid of action.

Rick couldn't help his smile. "Thanks, dude. You might have just saved my life."

~ * ~

Those one hundred and thirty minutes nearly killed him, but Rick made it. He powered through the torturous end of his workday one minute at a time, just like how he'd gotten through BUD/S and later Green Team training to become a DEVGRU

SEAL.

He'd learned early the only way to swallow Hell was one bite at a time.

Before Rick knew it, he was pulling his truck into his driveway. As much as he wanted to get to Jon's, even if he would be way early, he wanted to change out of his damn uniform first.

If Rick was going to successfully pretend his life was anywhere close to what it had been when he was in the teams, it couldn't be while he was wearing the vestiges of his dreaded day job.

He was coming to hate the stiff navy blue polyester shirt and matching pants and the black gum-soled shoes.

When he'd been crawling through the mountains of the border provinces in Afghanistan, sneaking up on possible insurgent strongholds in the dead of night, he never thought he'd miss the pounds of body armor or the weapons that weighed him down. Damned if he didn't miss it all now.

But Jon had called a GAPS meeting and that was like a light at the end of a dark tunnel. That propelled Rick into the house with a quick stride.

"Where are you in such a hurry to get to?" Darci called after him from the kitchen when he was already through his bedroom door.

"Jon's," he yelled back.

He felt a mean but justifiable satisfaction Darci couldn't be there for the meeting because it was at Jon's condo.

Last time GAPS had met here at their house, Darci had ended up going on the damn job with Chris instead of Rick. And it was at a resort in

Florida.

Darci, who had no training in anything other than banking, had gone on his mission. All while Rick, with years of SOF training, had gotten to go to his boring job.

While Chris and Darci had been treated to an all-expenses paid trip to a ritzy resort in the Florida Keys, he'd been cooling his heels in the cold dank Virginia February weather.

As Chris got to single-handedly save the resort's yacht and all of its passengers when it had been hijacked, Rick got to watch monitors and make hourly rounds of the nuclear facility.

That was not going to happen again. Rick was not going to sit the next mission out. He didn't care if he ended up owing his soul and every one of his days off for the next year to Mike for covering for him at the plant to do it. It would be worth it to see some real action.

He pulled off his ID badge and tossed it onto the dresser. The weapon came off next. That was the only thing about this job he liked—he got to carry a gun.

It wasn't like the kickass, customized weapons he'd had at his disposal as a DEVGRU SEAL. The handgun was like a peashooter in comparison to what he'd become used to, but hell, at least it was something.

Darci wandered to his doorway. "What's going on at Jon's?"

He glanced at her and then back to his dresser, where he pulled open a drawer and grabbed a shirt.

"Meeting."

"For GAPS?"

"Yes, and no you can't come."

"Why not?"

Rick didn't have to turn around to know she was unhappy. He heard it in her tone.

He shot her a glare over his shoulder. "Because in spite of you going on that one—and only one mission—you are not a team member."

The resurgence of the topic got him pissed off all over again. His sister had been on more missions than he had in the past month. Okay, it was only one, but in this case, one was too many.

"Is it secret or something?"

"No." Rick realized he wasn't sure of that answer and backpedaled. "I don't know. Maybe. Jon didn't say in the text."

"He must have texted Chris too. Because Chris texted me and said he couldn't come over tonight."

Ah, ha. So that was it. Darci was at loose ends because Chris was going to be busy tonight. His sister got bored easily. Hell, it must be hereditary.

Rick turned to face Darci. If she was going to leave him alone so he could shower and get dressed to go to Jon's, he figured he was going to have to finish this conversation with her.

He sighed. "Why don't you call Ali? She'll have nothing to do either since Jon is busy."

Darci lifted one shoulder. "I guess I could give her a call. We haven't hung out and had a night, just girls, in awhile."

"Sounds good. I'm going to take a shower." Standing with his clean clothes in one hand, he waited. When Darci still didn't move, he said, "Go call Ali."

If she was procrastinating and waiting for him to suggest she come with him to Jon's for this GAPS meeting, she would be waiting for a very long time because that was not gonna happen. Besides, if Jon had wanted females there, he would have invited them. He hadn't and that was just fine with Rick.

This meeting, this assignment, was going to be his if he had any say in it. Selfish bastard that he was, he wasn't sharing it.

CHAPTER FOUR

"I wanna go *out*." Sierra heard the underlying whine in her own tone, but she didn't care.

"You can't go out until the security team is in place."

"It's not like I want to go clubbing. Just let me go for a run." She needed to expend some of the nervous energy and get out of the hotel before she lost her mind.

"Use the gym here."

"I hate the treadmill. You know that. I want to be outside."

"Sierra, you're acting as if I've had you locked away in a dungeon for a month instead of in a luxury suite in a hotel for one day. Just hang on a little while longer."

It didn't matter how nice of a place Roger was keeping her in, she was still a prisoner there. Pouting wouldn't help. Whining wouldn't either.

She needed to reason with him. Appeal to his good sense.

"Look, Roger, we already met with the police and filed all the reports. The hotel knows what's happening and they say they've beefed up security."

She'd repeated the details, what few she had, ad nauseam. Sierra had told the story of the mysterious envelope appearing in her trailer to every uniformed person who'd asked.

"That's exactly right. The hotel is taking extra precautions, so you need to stay here, in the hotel, where you're safe. Until we get your personal security in place no going outside."

"You mean get my new watchdog over here." She scowled over the thought of the bodyguard Roger was forcing on her.

"A dog would be good actually. I'll contact the company I hired and see if they have guard dogs."

Sierra rolled her eyes at Roger. "I was kidding."

"Yes, I know, Sierra, but I wasn't." Roger raised his coffee cup to his lips, shooting her a glare over the top as he drank.

"I know that and that's exactly what scares me."

He was going to have her watched day and night, at work and at home.

Roger taking this so seriously made Sierra have to think about the situation she'd rather ignore. And now, on top of that stress, she was going to have some stuffy Secret Service wannabe following her around.

Or worse, some muscle-bound, bouncer-type bruiser who had more brawn than brains.

Neither scenario was appealing.

Thanks to Roger's insistence, once her human watchdog arrived, it would be a full twenty-four/seven with no private time to herself. That would be a living hell.

Maybe the police would have some leads on who had sent those pictures soon. That was the only hope to end this nightmare.

"What if I got a gun?" The idea hit her from out of the blue.

Her announcement must have hit Roger just as suddenly. He choked as he swallowed his coffee. "Excuse me?"

"If I had a gun, I could protect myself. I wouldn't need your guard. If I got some sort of holster, I could bring it with me while I was out for a run—"

"No. Definitely not."

"Why not?"

He shook his head, looking more distraught. Why? She'd come up with what seemed like a really good solution to the problem.

"Sierra, this person could be crazy. They could drive up next to you and throw you in the back of a van before you ever got your gun out of your jogging holster."

Just what she needed—the image of being kidnapped and thrown into a windowless van. "Thanks so much for putting that very vivid visual into my head."

"You needed me to. Sugarcoating this won't do you any good."

"You've never sugarcoated anything in your life."

"Nope. That's why you are where you are." Roger reached out and squeezed the back of her neck. "And why you love me."

"You're lucky I do love you or you'd be on the unemployment line."

"Yeah, yeah. I know."

"I still want a handgun."

"And I want a month off in Tahiti with those hottie male strippers from *Magic Mike*. I figure we both have about equal chance of getting what we want."

Sierra tipped her head to one side. "Well, I do know the casting director who worked on that movie so . . ."

"No gun, sweetie."

"Can we just go to the store and look at—"

"No. I'm going to make a few phone calls and see what's happening with that security. You relax. Go take a bath or something." He pressed a kiss to her head and in essence, dismissed her like she was a child.

Relax. Ha! Not much chance of that happening while he was on the phone checking on the ETA of her bodyguard to protect her from her stalker.

Sierra moved to the window in the living area. The curtains were closed tightly making the room feel dark in spite of the lamps being on. The whole room felt smaller and stifling but Roger had insisted the curtains remain closed and the police had agreed.

She used one finger to separate the edges of the two curtains just a crack and peered through. It was late enough in the evening that it was dark outside.

That made her feel moderately better. It felt worse being cooped up when the sun was shining brightly.

Was he there, outside, watching? He might be.

He or *she*, Sierra reminded herself. There was nothing proving the photographer was a man. It could be a woman.

What motivation did this person have? Hate? Love? Obsession?

Freaked out now, just from thinking about what might be going on in the mind of her stalker, she let the curtain fall back into place. She stepped back farther into the room and away from the window.

Roger stepped up behind her. "He'll be here tonight."

"Tonight?" Surprised, she turned to face Roger. She'd figured this person would start work in the morning.

"Yes. They're taking this seriously, Sierra. As you should be."

That strange sensation, the same feeling of doom she had when she first saw that envelope in her trailer, still niggled in the back of her brain. Whatever sixth sense she had, she had to learn to trust it. She was going to heed it this time.

She turned toward Roger. "Okay. I will. I do."

He lifted a brow. "You'll cooperate with them? Do what they say?"

God, how she hated being told what to do.

"Yes." That she'd agreed proved to her, and probably to Roger as well, exactly how unsettled she was.

CHAPTER FIVE

When everyone who was coming was there, including Zane who'd just strolled in, Jon opened his notebook on the table. "So we've got two things on tonight's agenda."

That there were two possible jobs for GAPS made Rick happy enough he could ignore his hatred of the concept of them having an agenda.

He'd gladly suffer through meetings and agendas if the end result was him on a mission, hopefully wearing a weapon a bit more exciting than the one he had for work, but he was in no position to be picky.

At this point he'd take what he could get in the action department.

Jon tapped the end of his pencil on the pad of paper as he glanced around the table. "First up, we got a consulting gig."

The joy bubbling inside Rick didn't diminish just

because the first job sounded more like they'd be pushing papers than pulling triggers. Consulting could be fun. It could entail live demos or training.

Using his own years of training to kick the ass of some green trainees—yeah, he could get into that.

"Where?" Rick asked, jumping the gun even though he was sure Jon would have gotten to that point eventually.

Jon's usual poker face broke. He grinned as he said, "The meeting's set for next week at Camp Lemonier."

"Djibouti?" Chris whooped at that announcement. "Hell, yeah."

Brody laughed. "Congrats, bro. That's huge."

Huge enough, even Zane put down his phone long enough to participate in the conversation. "Yes, sir. We're being brought in as civilian contractors to analyze and advise. They're moving the protection and education of ships' crews in the Gulf of Aden to the private sector. Piracy in that area is actually on the decline the past couple of years. And the military is a little busy at the moment with the current situation in Yemen."

"Yeah, I guess all out civil war just a few miles across the water is enough to get the big guys' attention."

Rick knew Brody was right. That a consulting job for GAPS, taking place at the Joint Task Force's base in Africa, was a huge step up. And if they landed the gig to train the shipping corporations' crews—a job like that could only help GAPS grow and move forward, but the reality was that this job did nothing for Rick's current malaise. He couldn't pick up and fly to the Horn of Africa, no matter how willing Mike had been to cover some extra shifts.

He rallied his support. What was good for the company was good for him. He'd have to repeat that mantra at his next shift at work.

Rick forced a smile. "That's great, man."

"Yeah, it's big. Which is why I was hoping we could all take a look at what information they sent us and do some prep work tonight, but then I got a call with a situation that needs to be handled immediately. He just called again right before Zane got here and he needs someone there like now."

Rick's happiness bubble re-inflated. "I can do it."

Jon lifted a brow. "You don't even know what it is."

"I don't care. Dude, if I don't get some action, things are going to get ugly."

"There's girls at the club just off base that can take care of that." Chris grinned.

Although he'd been lacking in that area too, Rick leveled a tolerant gaze at his friend. "That's not the kind of action I'm talking about."

Ignoring the exchange about strippers, Jon asked, "What's your availability?"

Rick was happy to inform him he was free and clear—at least for the near future. "I'm off for the next two days and after that I can probably get coverage."

"All right. It's yours."

The smile was too huge for Rick to even try and control it, not that he wanted to. He was happy to have a mission and he didn't care who knew it.

"What are the details?" Rick asked.

"Basic close protection. Twenty-four seven for an indeterminate amount of time," Jon began.

His mind spun with the possibilities. The client might be a politician who wasn't eligible for Secret Service protection so was hiring from the private sector. That was probably the case. Besides the fact that Zane had political connections, GAPS was located near enough to Washington, D.C. they should probably expect to get a lot of politicians for clients.

Jon continued, "As far as I can tell it'll only require one man on at a time. You and Chris should be able to handle it even while Zane and I are in Djibouti. Between all of us, we should be able tag team this thing and take shifts to make sure she's covered at all times."

"She?" That little detail piqued Rick's curiosity further.

One glance around the table told him that Chris and Brody's interest in the details of this assignment had heightened as well.

Zane shook his head. "Now you've really got their attention."

"Yeah, I see that." Jon let out a snort.

"So who is this mysterious *she*?" Chris asked.

"You ever hear of Sierra Cox?" Jon asked.

"You mean Sierra Cox the actress?" Chris asked as Rick's eyes widened at the thought.

"That's the one." Jon nodded.

"Uh, yeah. I've heard of her." Chris shot Rick a glance before looking back to Jon. "That's who this security gig is for?"

"Yup." Jon turned to Rick. "You up for this?"

"Why wouldn't I be?" He wasn't sure if he should be insulted by that question or not.

"Because she's got a bit of a reputation for being . . . difficult." Zane's tone hinted at the challenge that would be facing them all as her security team.

"More difficult than that ass of a general we had to escort around Ramadi because he wanted a tour of the hot zone?" Brody's question raised a memory they all shared.

It was an event that had taken place years ago when they'd all been on active duty. Before Chris had retired. Before Rick's knee blew out. Before Jon and Zane had turned in their paperwork to try and make a go of it as private military contractors.

Jon grinned. "Probably about the same, I'm guessing."

Chris chuckled. "Makes sense. One diva is just like another, right?"

The truth was, Rick didn't care how difficult this Sierra Cox was. It was a mission and he was happy to have it. Rick leaned forward. "You said they want us to start immediately?"

"Yup." Jon dipped his head. "Her manager just called to confirm."

Rick eyed Jon's notebook on the table. "Write down the details. I'm ready to go."

Truer words had never been spoken. He was more than ready to get started on this assignment, and only a small portion of that anticipation had to do with the fact he'd be guarding the body of the person named last year's Sexiest Woman on Earth.

CHAPTER SIX

The knock on the door interrupted Sierra's attempt at finding peace and quiet in the midst of this stalker hell that had become her reality . . . that is if she could call the noise a knock.

It was much more like a pounding. One so loud she heard it all the way from the bathtub in her suite.

"Roger? Are you out there?" She yelled the question through the closed bathroom door but since the noise continued, she had to assume he'd gone.

He had said he might run downstairs to grab a Starbucks quick while she tried to relax in the tub.

When he'd second-guessed that decision, saying he was afraid to leave her alone even for a few minutes before the security got here, she'd insisted he was crazy. She was locked in not just the suite, but also in the bathroom. What could happen?

Since the relaxation portion of her bath was definitely done now after the interruption, she sighed and heaved herself out of the water.

It had begun to get too cool for her taste anyway. Give her a scorching bath and she was a happy girl.

Standing, she reached for the towel as the water dripped off her skin tinged pink from the hot bath.

As the pounding continued, she opened the bathroom door and shouted, "One minute!"

Whoever was at the door might not be able to hear her but it was the best she could do at the moment. She wrestled the robe hanging on the back of the door over her wet arms and tied the belt tight as the pounding, thankfully, stopped.

"About time." She mumbled the complaint under her breath to the empty room as she padded barefoot past the king-size bed and through the door into the living room of the suite.

The sound of a keycard in the lock of the door leading to the hall had her stopping dead in her tracks. It could be Roger, coming back in. But he wouldn't have knocked. He had a key.

What if it was her stalker? He could have been knocking to see if she was inside and alone. Now that it was apparent she was, he was coming in. He could have knocked Roger out and taken his key. Or possibly stolen a master key from housekeeping.

Horrible scenarios flew through her head as she stood and waited, helpless, for the door to open and reveal who was on the other side. What fate awaited her.

Panicked, she looked for the nearest object she could use to defend herself. The lamp on the desk was glass. That would just break over the stalker's head and make him madder.

Why was there no pointy, metal letter opener? Then she could stab—

"Hello?" The deep male voice had her heart stopping.

"I have a gun. Don't come any closer." She was an actor, and a good one, so the idle threat sounded authentic to her. And dammit, tomorrow she was getting herself a gun for real. She didn't care what Roger said about it.

Whoever it was must have believed her lie about the gun. The door to the hallway remained partly open, but he didn't walk through. He stayed shielded safely behind the heavy wood. "Ms. Cox. I'm Rick Mann from GAPS."

What the fuck was GAPS? "I don't care who you are. Why do you have a key to my room?"

"I met with your manager in the lobby. He gave me a key. Look, if I could just come in—"

"No! Stay where you are. I'm calling Roger."

"Sierra, I'm right here." Roger's voice had her able to breathe again, but she was no less angry and her heart continued to pound.

"Why did you give him a key?" She frowned at her manager as he came through the door, followed by a hulk of a man who dwarfed him in height and size.

"Because he's going to need one if he's going to be coming in and out with you for the foreseeable future." Roger's calm demeanor about a strange, not to mention large man coming into her suite while she was in the tub made Sierra madder.

"*If* is the operative word in that statement. I haven't decided if I'll be going with his services." She spat the words as she eyed the man, who had gone from watching the exchange between her and Roger to visually surveying the room.

"I can assure you he's more than qualified." As Roger spoke, this Rick person closed the door to the hallway.

"Hold on. I didn't say you could stay."

"You can decide if I stay or go while the door is secured. There's someone at least watching you, possibly out to harm you. Let's not leave the door open for him to do it, okay?"

The hulk was right, of course, but for some reason that only pissed her off. "Fine."

He moved farther into the room, heading for the windows. Lifting the curtain, he glanced outside, before letting it fall back into place and adjusting it so there was no crack visible between the two panels. He glanced up at the ceiling, squinting at the smoke detector mounted there.

When he pulled a chair over and stood on it to get a closer look at the mechanism, she couldn't keep quiet any longer. "What are you doing?"

"Checking for surveillance." He glanced in her direction before focusing on dismantling the hotel's property.

"Holy shit. I never even considered that." Roger sighed. "See, Sierra. This is why we need him and his company."

"Be careful. They'll probably charge me for that if you break it."

"I won't break it." This time he didn't even look

at her when he spoke, which was probably better since there were now wires hanging out of the ceiling.

"If you get electrocuted, it's not my fault."

He laughed, surprising her. Then, the device was back where it belonged. Intact and looking none the worse for his tampering. Even the little red light was blinking away as usual.

Rick stepped down off the chair and moved it back to where he'd gotten it. "Finished and without being electrocuted. Sorry to disappoint you." He turned to Roger. "There's no camera in that, but I'd like to bring in equipment and sweep the room for anything that I might miss in a manual inspection."

Roger's eyes widened. "You think someone might have planted a bug in here?"

The blond beast dipped his head. "It's possible. That's how they could be getting tipped off as to her schedule and movements. People move easily in and out of hotel rooms. House keeping. Maintenance. Anyone could have been in here while you all were out."

And Roger had accused her of being paranoid in the past? This guy took the prize for paranoia.

"Mr. Mann, no one has to bug my room to know my schedule. Between fans and paparazzi, my every move is broadcast all over social media in seconds."

He lifted one shoulder, as if he was too lazy for a full shrug. "I'd think that would be one reason why you'd at least want privacy in your own room."

"Bring in the equipment." As Roger authorized this sweep, Sierra had to think that bugs—of the surveillance variety, not the other kind—would be less intrusive than Mr. Six-Foot-Five here.

Even if he did have blue eyes and blonde hair and muscles that made his short-sleeved collared shirt fit a little too tightly.

Men like him were a dime a dozen in Hollywood and not a one had ever tempted her. Sierra knew from personal experience that there was always some flaw. A huge deal breaker that made the single life preferable to pairing off with any one of them.

Mostly, they were assholes.

Her personal guard dog sure had a cocky aura blaring off him like a bad stink.

One thing she hated was a man who acted like a know-it-all. And worse than that was one who was a dummy and still acted superior to her, all because he was bigger and stronger because he had more muscles than she did.

She wasn't going to put up with it. Not in her own home—or her home away from home for the remainder of this shoot.

"I'll call now and see about getting that equipment over here." Mr. Mann, who was so obviously overfilled with testosterone even his name reiterated his masculinity, moved to the other side of the room to make a call on his cell phone.

Sierra moved closer to Roger. "Where did you get this guy?"

"Guardian Angel Protection. They're a local company."

Local. That figured. She scowled. "No doubt."

"They have excellent references."

"You checked?" she asked.

"Of course, I checked." A deep furrow creased

Roger's brow. "I even spoke to someone in Senator Greenwood's office in Washington just to be sure. This is your safety we're talking about here, Sierra. I'm taking it very seriously. And so is the owner of the security company, which is why he agreed to get someone here tonight, rather than tomorrow."

She shrugged. "It's not like we needed him here tonight. I'm just going to go to bed early."

"And won't you sleep better knowing he's out here, on watch? I know I sure will."

"He's going to be right here in my living room all night long?" Outside in the hallway would be fine, but a stranger inside her suite was too close for comfort.

"Yes, Sierra. That's what round the clock protection entails. Day and night. I thought you understood that."

"I guess I didn't consider all the implications."

Roger shook his head, before he drew her to him in a hug. "You don't have to. That's why I'm here."

"You, and now my own personal Ken doll on steroids with an attitude."

Roger's eyes widened. "I know, right? He is Ken doll cute but with a GI Joe kind of edge to him."

Sierra let out a laugh. "Then maybe you should stay here all night too. You know, to supervise his performance."

"I wish." Roger glanced at the brute on the phone and then sighed. "Unfortunately, I don't think he's interested in me."

"The only thing he does seem interested in is surveillance equipment, so don't feel bad. In fact, he's so damn perfect, maybe he's a cyborg or something."

Roger chuckled. "Hey, if this drought in my love life continues for much longer, a cyborg might be an option."

"You work too hard. That's your problem."

He lifted a brow. "Sorry. Can't help that. My boss is a slave driver."

Sierra snorted. "If I was in charge around here, GI Joe wouldn't currently be inspecting my heating unit while on the phone ordering a delivery of bug detection equipment like it's a pizza."

Roger turned to her. "You had to say that? Now I want pizza. We never got around to having dinner."

She laughed. "Might as well order one. Or better make it two. I bet Mr. Manly-Man eats a lot."

That was the only way to get muscles that large. Lots of food, in addition to pumping iron for hours a day. The bastard could probably eat all the carbs he wanted and not gain an ounce of fat.

Sierra resented the massive intrusion in her life for a whole new reason now.

The thought of having him outside her door all night long while she was trying to sleep had her craving comfort food in massive amounts. But the knowledge of what carbs did to her body had her saying to Roger, "Order me a salad along with that pizza."

"You got it." Roger whipped out his cell phone while Sierra watched the new man in her life continue to hold a conversation she couldn't hear with someone on his cell phone.

He was a fine specimen. Probably nothing between the ears, but from the neck down his muscles were enough to have her remembering keenly how long it had been since she'd had a steady boyfriend. And in her position, one-night stands were out of the question.

Nope. Her life in the public spotlight meant she couldn't gain even an ounce without speculation in the tabloids that she had a *baby bump*.

Sierra sighed with frustration. No good food. No sex. No life.

She did have some really great shoes though. That counted for something. Right?

CHAPTER SEVEN

Rick listened to the ringing through the earpiece of his cell until he heard Jon, when he finally answered, say, "Hey, Rick. You at the hotel?"

"I am." Rick heard the ambient noise on the other end of the line. "The guys still at your place?"

"Yup. Unfortunately, we seem to have moved on from planning our presentation in HOA to plotting how to get more beer over here without any of us having to go out and get it."

He knew these guys, as well as if they were his blood brothers, and that sounded about right to him.

A discussion about Jon and Zane's presentation in Djibouti would naturally lead to memories of when they'd all been stationed on the Horn of Africa in the SEAL encampment on Camp Lemonier. And memories inevitably were accompanied by a cold one—or six.

Rick laughed. "You know, one call to Darci and

she'll deliver it to you."

"You think?" Jon asked.

"I don't just think, I *know*. She was dying to get over to your place for that GAPS meeting."

"Really? Why?" Jon sounded surprised.

He shouldn't be. He'd been the one to approve Darci going on that mission with Chris. He should have known after one she'd want another. Action was addicting—an obsession Rick knew too well.

Rick would happily remind his friend whose fault this was. "This one's all on you, bro. Since you sent her on that one job, she thinks she's an operative now. But hey, you tell her you need supplies for the planning meeting and she'll be in her car so fast your head'll spin."

Jon let out a chuckle. "Okay, thanks. I'll keep that in mind. How's it going there with you?"

How to answer that? Rick was there. He'd met the clients. He liked Roger well enough. But Sierra "Diva" Cox—she was another story altogether.

"It's . . . uh, going."

There was a silent pause from Jon's end of the line in response to Rick's skirted honesty. "You do realize that answer doesn't exactly instill confidence, right?"

Time to tap dance and reassure his boss things were fine. Which they were, even if Ms. Cox kept shooting daggers at him with those angry emerald-colored eyes of hers.

Rick's first GAPS assignment was not going to get derailed by a diva, even if she was centerfold-worthy. He didn't care what he had to do. Hell, he'd spit shine her shoes if it made her happy but he was not failing and letting Jon or GAPS down.

"Nah. It's fine. I'm good. Just never been in a hotel suite this fancy before. I guess I'm a little tongue tied. The living room in this place is bigger than mine and Darci's whole house."

Jon snorted. "Yeah, well it probably costs more a night than your mortgage every month so don't be too jealous."

He hadn't considered that but, of course, Jon was probably right about that. Diva was hella rich.

No wonder she was so stuck up. She couldn't help it.

Rick allowed himself to digest that for just a second before work-mode took over. "So how is GAPS set up as far as surveillance-detection equipment goes?"

"Oh, well let me just take a look at our latest equipment warehouse inventory." Jon paused, no doubt for dramatic effect to complement his sarcasm. "Rick, right now we're buying equipment as we need it. I mean we got the essentials necessary for a QRF kit—weapons, ammo, vests and plates, but specialty stuff, like what you're asking about, we'll have to go buy."

"Oh. That's okay. I guess I don't need—"

"Rick. No. That's not what I meant. I don't stockpile this stuff, but if you need it, I'll happily get it."

"You sure? I can make do with a manual sweep." Rick knew GAPS hadn't scored a whole lot of work in its brief history. He felt bad asking Jon to spend any of their initial investment that could go toward more important needs, such as beefing up their

Quick Reaction Force kits. Or buying those four-tube NVGs he'd been jonesing for Jon to get for the team.

"The client is paying us a nice sum for this gig and we've got money in the bank. Besides, a bug detector is probably something we'll get a lot of use out of. It's all good. I'll call around. If I can't find any place open tonight, I'll get it in the morning and run it over to you."

"That would be great. Thanks, Jon."

"No problem. I'd like to meet the client in person anyway."

"Yup. You probably should." Rick tempered his reply and didn't issue the warning that was on the tip of his tongue.

He glanced across the room as Ms. Cox, with her chestnut hair piled up on top of her head.

A fluffy white robe dwarfed her, its color a stark contrast to the heightened hue of her cheeks.

Crap, she was looking too sexy for her to be a client. Why couldn't he have gotten some old governmental dude to guard instead?

This was his first big assignment for GAPS. He needed his head in the game, not on wondering what was under that robe.

If he hadn't taken the time to look her up online before coming over, the image of her in a bikini wouldn't be flashing through his sex-deprived brain.

That was sad recompense for doing his due diligence. He should have just driven over unprepared. He would have been better off blissfully ignorant to what Sierra Cox's smooth lean limbs looked like, bronzed and oiled in that photo spread.

He had to stop thinking like that or he'd embarrass himself and probably get GAPS fired from what was a pretty primo job.

Meanwhile, any fantasies on Rick's part would remain just that. Fantasy.

Mainly because he had to be professional but also because there was no way Sierra Cox wanted anything to do with him. Not professionally or personally.

That was clear by the attitude radiating off her from across the room. She might be swaddled in fluff, but she sure as hell had a demeanor that was hard as nails.

Sierra was like an overwhelming spitfire compressed in a deceivingly small and sweet-looking package. Kind of like that chocolate-covered fire ant he ate on a dare when they'd all been in HOA.

That had been the easiest fifty bucks he'd ever made. Unfortunately, Rick had a feeling conquering Sierra Cox would not be so easy.

CHAPTER EIGHT

For what had to be the dozenth time Sierra glanced at the clock.

Sleep eluded her, and it wasn't because of the potentially deadly, camera-wielding stalker, or the possibility of a bug being planted in her suite to monitor her every move. It was without a doubt the fact that even her unconscious brain was very aware of—not to mention disturbed by—the presence of the bruiser in her living room.

The ceiling was too boring to stare at any longer so Sierra closed her eyes and prayed for sleep. Sleep that didn't come.

She should have taken a sleeping pill. Unfortunately she needed a full eight, and ideally nine hours of sleep to not feel like a zombie in the morning. She had to be at the studio at nine a.m. for hair and makeup.

One glance at the numbers glowing on the

bedside clock told her it was far too late to take anything now. Anything other than a shot of alcohol, that is.

Maybe she should raid the minibar. Drink enough to put her in a drunken coma for the next— how many hours? She did a quick calculation in her head. The answer wasn't good.

To shower, dress and get to the lot in time, she'd have to get up in two and a half hours. Three if she really rushed her morning routine and ate breakfast in the makeup chair.

But if she was going to be sleep deprived because of this Rick person thrust upon her, she certainly hoped he would be too. Not that it mattered. He didn't have to look fresh and pretty on camera tomorrow. He didn't have to remember lines and blocking cues.

Was he even awake out there? Was he sitting up, watching the door and windows with an eagle eye, ready to pounce at any sign of an intruder? Or, and this was far more likely in her opinion, was he stretched out, sleeping on the sofa that would no doubt be too short for him?

The curiosity ate at her until she was more awake than before. There was no freaking way she had any hope of dozing now. Not until she had an answer to her question.

She flipped the covers back and swung her legs over the side of the mattress. Bare-footed, Sierra padded across the plush carpet, guided by the light from the living room that slipped through the crack between the door and the frame.

Foiled by the fact the space was too small for her

to peek through, she turned the knob, slowly in an attempt to be silent and sneak up on him.

It didn't work. The moment the door opened, he glanced up from his seat on the sofa and smiled. "Good morning."

Sierra couldn't have frowned any deeper. "Morning? How is this morning?"

His cell phone was already in his hand. He hit a button and turned it to face her to display the time. "It's five. That's morning."

"How can you consider five a.m. morning? The sun isn't even up. Is it?" She generally made it to about closing time of whatever club she happened to be partying at, and then went straight to bed. So five in the morning was uncharted territory for her.

The bastard managed to look handsome even at this ungodly hour as he grinned at her. "The sun doesn't necessarily dictate when morning starts. There were days I'd get in my run, shower, and eat breakfast all before the sun came up."

That confirmed her suspicions. He was a health nut.

"That's very admirable." She complimented him, but the sarcasm in her tone was pretty clear.

She should probably be more careful how she spoke, given he was in possession of a gun. She hadn't noticed it before, but there it was, on the table next to him.

"Coffee?" He stood and grabbed the gun, sliding it into a hidden ankle holster before letting his pant leg slide back into place.

After witnessing that disturbing move, she somehow found the words to ask, "You made coffee?"

"Yup. Brewed a fresh pot about half an hour ago. Should still be plenty fresh, even for *your* taste buds."

There was an insult in there but she was too flabbergasted to respond to it.

She shouldn't be standing in front of him in what she was wearing at all, never mind having coffee with this guy. She glanced down at her attire. She was wearing men's style silk pajamas so she was covered, technically. But the fabric was so thin and clingy she might as well have been wearing gauze. He'd be able to see every jiggle, every pucker . . . and damn why were her nipples hard?

"I didn't think it was that hard of a question." His comment brought her back to the issue at hand—his offer of coffee.

Crossing her arms over her chest, she glanced up to see him watching her, coffee pot in hand. She needed to answer him. She also needed to go put on a bra. "Um, yeah. Sure. I'll be right back."

He reached for another cup. "Okay. Cream? Sugar?"

She'd already gone in the bedroom, but his words followed her inside. Poking her head out through the doorway, she called back, "I'll fix it myself. Just leave it there."

"All right. I probably couldn't have gotten it right anyway."

Another dig from the brute, thinly veiled as him trying to be helpful. Unable to let this one go, even as she wrestled to get her bra on, she called through the closed door, "Probably not."

By the time she got her pajama top back on, over the bra this time, and emerged from the bedroom, he was back on the sofa. This time, there was a coffee mug in one hand and his cell phone in the other.

She headed toward the coffee maker. "What is so interesting on that phone of yours? You updating the *Guardian Angels With Guns* Facebook page?"

Guardian Angels, her ass. Fallen Angels more like, judging by the looks of him. She smiled at her own cleverness as she reached for the artificial sweetener Roger had stocked in the kitchenette for her. Maybe she'd hold on to that Fallen Angel dig and use it the next time he insulted her.

"No. Jon's girlfriend Ali handles our social media. He's the founder. You'll meet him today. He's supposed to be dropping off the equipment I asked for sometime this morning." He shot her a glance as she wandered over to the seating area with her coffee mug. "And you can call it GAPS for short. Guardian Angels with Guns is such a mouthful. I do like it though."

His grin deflated her whole dig. It was no fun when the subject of her mocking enjoyed it. He even chuckled at the name, before he lifted his phone again.

"What are you reading on there?"

"Sun Tzu."

"Sun Tzu, as in *The Art of War*?" Her eyes widened, but her shock at his reading at all, and something without pictures in it, didn't last long. It was soon replaced by her anger when he acted more surprised than she had.

His sandy colored brows rose above his blue eyes. "You've heard of it?"

"Of course I've heard of it. What's shocking is that *you're* reading it."

"Eh, you don't know me very well, so I'll give you a pass for acting ignorant."

Again, the insult had rolled off the blond brute like water off a duck's back. Amusing him rather than pissing him off, which was rapidly becoming her goal—to make him as angry as he made her, seemingly without much effort at all.

He lowered the phone again, probably after realizing she was sitting there scowling at him.

What else could he expect her to do at five in the frigging morning besides sit there like a zombie barely able to hold her coffee mug?

Maybe he thought she'd go for a run like he bragged about doing before sun up daily.

Actually, that was a good idea. Roger couldn't stop her from going outside if she had her watchdog with her.

"So what are the plans for this morning?" he asked.

He laid the phone on the table in the vacant spot where the gun had been and she was reminded once more what kind of heat this man was packing.

"We have to be to the movie lot by nine."

He dipped his head. "All right. That's easy enough. It's a seven-minute drive. Accounting for morning traffic, we should head down to the car no later than eight-forty-five. Though earlier would be preferable."

How the hell?

Nope, she wasn't even going to question how he knew the exact amount of time to the minute it would take to drive to the set. She'd already concluded the reason. This man was obviously an obsessive-compulsive maniac.

But her stalker probably had the same character traits. He or she would have to have, to be able to track her movements, to be able to take those pictures and then know how to deliver them directly to her without being detected.

Fine. If it took one whacko to catch another one, she'd deal with it and him, and his gun, and his smart-ass comments, and all the rest.

She'd also use him to her own advantage. "I want to go for a run."

Not at this very moment, but shortly. She was still having trouble getting moving and as far as she knew, it was still dark outside those blackout curtains he had drawn so tightly.

A crease formed in his brow. "Um, let's table that for now."

"What?" She thought for sure he'd be all over it. Mr. I-Jog-Ten-Miles-Before-Sunrise wasn't into taking a run? She narrowed her eyes. "Did Roger get to you?"

He shook his head. "No, he didn't say anything about it. I need to check out the area first. Plan a secure route. Assess any areas that might pose a problem. Minimize the chance of a threat."

Sierra rolled her eyes. It was becoming apparent that everything was going to be like a full-scale mission with this guy, requiring planning to the tiniest detail.

She let out a frustrated sigh. "Fine."

"I'm sure this hotel has a gym you can use."

"I hate running on a treadmill." It came out a bit whiny.

She raised her eyes to his, expecting to see him looking amused that she had sounded like a child. Instead, she was surprised to see what looked like understanding in his expression.

"Me too. I'll talk about it with Jon and see what I can do. We might be able to get a run in later today. Maybe at the studio lot, if nothing else. That'll be easier to secure than the streets outside the hotel. Bring your running gear with you, okay?"

Hating that he'd actually come up with a viable and even creative solution to her problem, because she really did not want to like this guy, Sierra nodded. "Okay."

His lips tipped up in a smile. "Good. See? A little communication is all it takes to keep us both happy."

That cocky assumption on his part had any charitable feelings she'd had toward him fleeing. "Oh believe me, Mr. Mann, I'm not happy about any of this."

"I'm well aware of that, Ms. Cox, but my job is to keep you safe, not to make you happy. Besides, I'm sure you have people on your payroll for that."

His self-aggrandizing made her want to knock the smirk right off his face with one well placed slap. He'd probably only laugh at her losing control. She had to remain as cold and unaffected as he did.

"Just so we understand each other, the sooner we find who sent me those pictures, the better. Because

I'll be more than happy to get you and your GAPS friends off my payroll."

"On that point, ma'am, we're in total agreement." His cell phone vibrated, stealing the thunder of any retort she might have been able to come up with before the distraction. He glanced at the screen and then up at her. "We're about to have company. You staying like that, or would you like to go and change?"

He cocked up one brow as he waited for her answer. That in itself was enough to decide for her. "This is my hotel room and I'll dress any way I please."

"All right." Smiling he moved to the door and unlocked the deadbolt and the security lock, before twisting the handle.

Two men, not quite but nearly equal to her guard in size and bulk, entered through the open door. They moved in sync, like they'd been trained to do so.

One let out a long slow whistle as he looked around the room, barely glancing at her, but seeming more intrigued with the flat screen television.

"Nice digs. When's my turn for a shift?" The first man asked in a Southern drawl so thick she would have assumed it was fake if this had been a movie set.

But no, sadly, this was her life, not a film.

"When I say it's your shift." Rick shook hands with him, and then with the other man. "What are you two doing here?"

"Jon was having trouble finding what you

needed, but I was able to, let's say *procure* the item you asked for." The second man spoke with an accent as heavy as the first.

Rick let out a low belly chuckle over whatever meaning he heard behind the words that she didn't hear. His gaze cut to her. "Sierra Cox, this is Brody Cassidy and his brother Chris. Chris works for GAPS."

Brothers. That explained it. Now that she looked at the two more closely, they resembled each other in more than just speech. They were also similar in their looks, and not just the hard toned bodies all three were sporting.

Muscles must be a requirement to get hired at this *Goon Angel Power Squad*. Amused at her new meaning for his GAPS acronym, Sierra tucked it away for future use.

The one named Chris tipped his head in her direction. "Nice to meet you."

Brody glanced up from pawing through the black bag he'd set on the side table long enough to say, "Ma'am." He turned his attention back to a device in his hand. "Let me show you how this one operates before we go."

The three huddled over the object and Sierra was left to watch and wonder what the hell was going on.

CHAPTER NINE

"Thanks for driving this over."

"No problem. Brody wanted to show you how to use the device so we told Jon we'd run it over."

"But it's like an hour drive."

"More like forty-five minutes with Brody here driving." Chris tipped his head toward his brother.

Brody's brows shot high. "I learned how to drive from you."

Chris wobbled his head, but didn't deny it. "Anyway, we're fixin' to head over to the airfield to take my plane up as long as we're in the area. So we got that fun today, in addition to the introduction to Miss Hot Pants of the Year."

"Technically, I think the title was sexiest woman of the year." Brody corrected his brother while all Rick could do was worry she was going to hear them and flip out.

"Keep it down. She's right there."

Chris raised a brow. "All the way across a room bigger than my house."

Brody let out a snort. "I know. Right? I really don't get paid enough. I get shot at with automatic weapons and RPGs and don't make probably an eighth of what she gets for getting shot with a camera."

"Speaking of, I need your opinion on something." Happy to move the conversation into safer territory, Rick raised his voice a bit now they'd be talking about something Sierra would be able to hear.

"Sure thing. *Shoot.*" Chris grinned at his own little joke.

Rick groaned at pun. "Anyway, she wants to go out for a run. What do you guys think?"

"Go for a run out there?" Chris hooked a thumb toward the window. "*Hell. No.*"

Rick knew it would be risky, but he didn't expect such an adamant response from Chris.

Brody shook his head. "I gotta agree. I wouldn't let her do it."

"Even if I scope it out in advance and go with her?" Rick asked.

"Nope. Not even then." Brody swung his head one more time.

The discussion had Sierra moving closer. She frowned. "Why not?"

Chris moved to the window and parted the curtains with one finger. "Because if it was me, I'd set up my hide on one of the higher floors of that tall building across the street. From there, I could have a bead on you from the moment you stepped outside, and up and down the street for a mile."

"Yup." Brody came up behind them. "And if he's set up on the rooftop, of course he'll be more exposed but he'll also have a view of both side streets and an even better shot."

"A *better shot* with his camera, you mean?" Sierra asked.

"Uh, yeah. That's what I meant. With his camera." Brody's eyes shifted to aim a sideways glance at Rick.

Sierra seemed to accept the lie at face value, even though it was so obviously not what Brody had meant.

It was a damn good thing she didn't know Chris was speaking as a veteran ST6 sniper and Brody as an active DEVGRU operative who currently held the kill record among the men in his unit.

Sometimes ignorance was bliss.

Rick didn't need Sierra scared out of her mind that he, Chris and Brody were talking about this stalker possibly carrying a gun rather than a camera. Being photographed without her knowledge had freaked her out enough.

As long as Rick and GAPS were on the job, she wouldn't need to know any of those things, or how much danger she might really be in.

He drew in a deep breath. "Okay, Ms. Cox here has a job to get to so let's sweep the bathroom and bedroom first so she can get ready."

"All righty. The bedroom it is." Chris grinned, acting his usual foolish self.

What Chris seemed to forget was that now Rick had a way to keep him in line. "Behave or I'll tell

Darci on you."

"Oh, that reminds me. Darci wants an autograph. You wanna ask Miss Sierra or should I?" Chris asked.

Rick rolled his eyes at the ridiculous request.

Enemy surveillance and snipers were all things he had been trained to deal with, but this job came with a whole other set of challenges. He'd battled sandstorms and heat, cold and snow, enemy fighters and warlords, but he'd be damned if he knew how to fight fame the likes of Sierra Cox's.

"Rick. You coming?" Brody's summons from the doorway of the bedroom knocked Rick out of his own head.

"Yeah. I'm coming." He paused by Sierra, standing in her pajamas, clutching her coffee mug and looking less than happy to have her privacy invaded further. "I'm sorry about this, but I'll feel a lot better after we sweep those rooms."

Her lips formed a tight line but she nodded her agreement.

That was probably all he could hope to get while there were three men, who were strangers to her, pawing through her bedroom and bathroom.

He decided to throw her a bone. "We'll take that run at the lot today. Okay?"

"Yeah, sure." She didn't even reward him with a smile.

Oh well. He'd tried.

"Fucking hell." The sound of Chris cussing in the next room had Rick running to catch up to them.

Tripping to a stop in the doorway between the bedroom and the bathroom, he saw Brody standing on the edge of the bathtub. The device he held up above his head was lit up like a damn string of Christmas tree lights.

Rick didn't need to ask what was wrong. He could figure that out all on his own. Brody had detected something in the ceiling tile. Something Rick had missed during his manual sweep last night.

Brody handed off the device to Chris and pressed against the ceiling tile with both palms. A few seconds later, he had the tile free of the supports. Tile in hand, Brody stepped down.

Both Chris and Rick moved in closer and they all saw what the device had detected.

"Pin hole camera stuck right in the damn acoustic tile." Brody grasped it between two fingers and squinted at it. "Looks like it's got a microphone built in too."

"Eyes and ears. He is one serious mother fucker." Chris shook his head.

Chris had it right. This was no amateur stalker with a cell phone camera. At the sound of a gasp, Rick turned and saw Sierra standing in the doorway, white faced and shaking.

Rick was shaken by the discovery himself. He could only imagine how badly Sierra was. But he was the professional here. It was his job to stay cool and, more importantly, keep her calm.

"You all right?"

She certainly didn't look all right. Rick took the coffee mug from her hand before she dropped it and put it on the vanity by the sink so he had two hands free to grip her arms. He steered her to the closed toilet seat and sat her down. The fact she let him, without argument, without even a smart comment, told him how shaken she truly was.

Squatting down in front of her brought them eye level, but she wasn't looking at him. She was staring off into space, her eyes focused on nothing, as if her mind rejected the idea someone had been watching and listening in on some very private situations.

Rick heard Chris on his cell phone, speaking softly to, no doubt, Jon. He'd need to be updated on this discovery. They'd have to ramp up security. That someone had gotten into her bathroom showed they had free access to the room. Possibly an employee with a master key.

Brody left the room and came back a minute later with a tiny bottle of whisky. He cracked the top and poured the contents into the cup of coffee, then handed it to Rick. "Get her to drink that. She's looking kinda shocky."

Rick didn't argue. The way she looked, trembling now like her blood had gone cold, a little liquor could only help. "Sierra. Drink this."

She shook her head.

"One sip. Come on. It'll make you feel better." He brought the mug closer to her lips.

Finally, she reached up and cupped it. He covered her shaking hands with his steady ones and helped guide the mug to her mouth.

She swallowed and wrinkled her nose.

"Don't tell me you're not a drinker. Party girl like you." Rick smiled when his comment had her eyes moving to shoot him a look from beneath lowered brows.

He preferred her pissed rather than the way she'd been just seconds ago.

Pocketing his phone, Chris moved closer to where Sierra sat with Rick in front of her. His gaze moved between the two. "Jon's on his way over. We're going to move you to another hotel."

"Where?" she asked.

"That's what we're going to figure out when he gets here. In the meantime, he doesn't think you should go to work today." Chris's suggestion stoked the fire in Sierra's eyes.

She shook her head. "No. I'm going to work. Do you know how much it would cost the studio if I chose to just not show up for a day?"

Chris lifted his brow. "No, ma'am. I can't say I do."

"I'm going to work." Her tone left no room for argument.

"All right." Rick nodded. "We'll sweep the area prior to your getting there. While you're at work, we can move your stuff to the new hotel *after* it's been swept and secured. Today will be just like any other day at work, except I'll be there with you."

She digested that for a minute. "Okay."

Her easy agreement was a pleasant surprise. One hurdle cleared.

Rick glanced up at Chris. "You okay with postponing that flight of yours?"

"No problem." Chris shifted his glance to Brody. "You feel like playing at being a GAPS employee for a little bit longer?"

Brody tipped his head. "Sure. It's turning out to

be more exciting than I'd anticipated."

Chris let out a snort. "Ain't that the truth."

Rick drew in a steadying breath. He had to agree with Brody and Chris.

This was turning into one hell of an assignment.

CHAPTER TEN

Once Sierra had gotten her legs to hold her weight and her hands to stop shaking long enough she could grip her cell phone, she called Roger. She didn't give a crap that it was six in the morning.

Even if it was the crack of dawn, she had a camera spying on her and, after the newest arrivals, nearly half a dozen men in her suite. She figured it was about time Roger got to share all the fun with her.

To his credit, he got to her room in just a few minutes, even though she could tell from his voice over the phone she'd woken him with her call.

After one of the two new arrivals opened the door at the sound of the knock, Roger came in, his concern evident from his expression.

He glanced in her direction, but paused to shake hands with the two men who'd introduced themselves as the founders of the company.

It was becoming difficult to keep all these guys and their names straight now that there were so many of them.

Looking at the security team now—all five standing together in a huddle on the other side of the room discussing her, no doubt—she came up with a new name for the company. GAPS could easily stand for *Glorious Abs and Pecs* from what she could see of the bulging muscles beneath their shirts.

She giggled at herself and wondered how much booze the one southern hottie had slipped into her coffee.

Finally, Roger broke away from the group and came over to her. His brow furrowed, he reached out to grab her hands. "Are you all right?"

"Yeah. I'm good."

He frowned deeper. "I don't know how you can be."

"One of the hard bodies over there put whisky in my coffee to calm me down. Where did you find these guys, anyway? The local male strip club?"

Roger's brows rose. "No. I told you, they're from a security company that was very highly recommended to me."

"I think they're clones."

"Why is that?"

"Look at them. Have you ever seen a group of men all in such good shape?"

"Yes." Roger smiled. "You should come to my gym. Why do you think I belong there? It's certainly not for the cardio class."

"So you think they're all gym rats?"

"Mm, no. We're very near Virginia Beach."

"So?"

"So, there are naval bases all around here. My guess is they're all former Navy."

Sierra wrinkled her nose. "I don't like that one white uniform sailors wear. It's the same outfit every mother of a three year old boy puts them in for pictures."

"Here's a little tip for you, sweetie. The uniform comes off." Roger focused his attention on the group of possibly former military bruisers across the room, proof of his admiration of the breed.

She eyed Roger. "You got a thing for sailors, do you?"

"Actually, he was a Marine but yeah, there's definitely something to be said for a man in uniform."

"And out of uniform?" Sierra suggested.

"Amen, sister." Roger grinned and then sobered as he turned back toward her. "But seriously, Sierra, you're too calm considering everything. They found a camera in your bathroom. Are you sure you're okay?"

No, not really.

"I just need to get to work and put it out of my mind."

She was scared. She was pissed. Knowing someone was watching her made her feel completely violated. But the fact that the camera was down now and in the hands of her watchdogs where it couldn't spy on her anymore helped.

That she'd be moving to a different hotel that would be checked out inch by inch by her super soldiers helped too.

Once she was on the lot, immersed in the life of her character and not her own, she'd be fine.

"You're probably right. Keeping busy will be better than sitting and obsessing over it." Roger evaluated her for a moment before nodding. "All right. I'll let you go to the lot."

Sierra widened her eyes. "Excuse me? You'll *let me*?"

Roger's lips twitched. "That's right. You pay me to tell you what to do, remember?"

"Yes. You make it hard to forget." She shot him an unhappy glance.

"Good." Roger looked much too satisfied with her acquiescence.

She didn't have time to discuss Roger or his acting like he was in charge. Rick and the dark-haired man who was his boss, broke from the group and came towards Sierra.

When he was right in front of her, Rick's blue-eyed gaze pinned Sierra, as if evaluating her. "You doing all right?"

Frustrated, she let out a huff of breath. "Yes. Everyone needs to stop asking me that question and instead work on catching this crazy person!"

"We're working on it. I'm meeting with hotel security today." The guy standing next to Rick— Jon, if she remembered correctly—joined the conversation.

"I thought you're moving me out of this hotel." She heard how high her tone rose as the panic filled her. There was no way she could sleep here tonight.

"We are moving you, and believe me that hotel

will be vetted from the housekeeping staff to the security protocols and the premises thoroughly swept before we move you in. I've already called the police officer in charge of your case and he'll be meeting with us as well. But we also have to get to the bottom of how someone gained access to your suite in this hotel."

Even though she wanted to hate these men and this company thrust upon her, Jon seemed capable and what he said made sense. Even as agitated as she was, she had to admit his plan, his words, calmed her a little bit.

"Okay."

"Chris and Brody are heading over to the studio." Jon's focus moved to Roger. "We're going to need them cleared at the gate and they'll need full access to the lot."

Roger reached into his pocket for his cell. "I'll call now and arrange it."

"Thanks." Jon turned back to address Sierra. "Zane's coming with me to handle the hotel situation. Rick's gonna stay with you."

Sierra nodded, in a daze from the sheer number of people involved in this, as much as from everything else that had happened, all before the sun had time to rise.

"I need something from you." Jon's stare was intense as it pinned her.

"What?"

"I need you to listen to what Rick says and do what he tells you."

That part, she didn't like. She frowned. "I don't—"

"Ms. Cox. Please. We can only keep you safe if you cooperate."

"I can handle this. I'm not as stupid as people think. I've dealt with pushy paparazzi and crazed fans for half of my life, all without the benefit of Rick telling me what to do."

"I never thought you were stupid. And I know this has been your life for a very long time. I'm well aware you were thirteen when you won the Academy Award for Best Supporting Actress—"

Her brows rose. "You did your homework."

"We always do. The point is, all of your experience doesn't include dealing with someone who is very possibly armed and dangerous. Rick has ten years dealing with high pressure, dangerous situations."

"Yeah, and he only got himself shot twice, was it?" Chris had wandered over to the conversation.

"It was three times, I thought." Brody grinned.

Rick scowled at the two brothers. "That third time was just shrapnel."

Chris lifted one shoulder. "You still bled all over the damn truck and I had to clean it up. Anyway, boss man, Brody and I are heading over to the lot."

Jon nodded. "I texted you the address."

"I got it. You arrange it so we can get in?" Chris asked.

Jon turned toward Roger for the answer to that question.

"It's all set," Roger answered.

Chris's gaze swung from his boss to Rick. "Your ETA still zero-nine-hundred?"

"That's when she's due in. We still on

schedule?" Rick asked Sierra.

In a daze, she nodded.

Chris slapped Jon on the back. "A'ight then. We'll be in touch."

Five men, six if she counted Roger, all coordinated to keeping her safe.

"I'm getting dressed." She made the announcement to no one in particular, more to the room in general and whoever might be listening. But before she turned to go into her room, she stopped. "There's no more cameras, right?"

"It's clean. I promise."

Choosing to believe Rick's answer, not because she trusted him but more because she wouldn't be able to function if she thought otherwise, she turned for her bedroom.

It was time to get on with her day. If she didn't, if she changed her life because of what was happening, it would mean he—or she—had won.

For better or worse, Sierra was too stubborn to let that happen.

CHAPTER ELEVEN

Rick sent Sierra a sideways glance as he waited for the line of traffic ahead to pull through the gate.

She'd surprised him by being dressed and ready to go long before the time they had to leave. Though maybe it wasn't such a surprise she wanted out of that hotel sooner rather than later.

"We're here like an hour early, you know," he said.

"I know." She hadn't bothered to look at him when she responded.

Instead, she stayed focused on something outside the passenger window.

She'd slipped on sunglasses when he'd told her they were driving over in his truck. Apparently being seen and recognized arriving in a pick-up was bad when you were Sierra Cox, so she was going incognito behind her shades.

Fine. Whatever floated her boat.

He turned his attention back to the line of cars in

front of him.

Getting onto this studio lot brought back bittersweet memories of driving onto base. There was always a line getting through the gate, especially in the morning.

The base traffic he could do without. Being active duty, though, *that* he missed. More than he realized. Having all the guys together again this morning assessing the threat, making a game plan like the old days when they'd been a team, had made him realize how much he missed it.

Finally, it was their turn. He rolled down the window. The guard leaned low, clipboard in his hand. "Name?"

Rick leaned back in his seat so the guard could see past him as he tipped his head toward his passenger. "Sierra Cox and her security."

The man nodded. "Pull through."

Rick took note that the rent-a-guard wasn't armed, from what he could see.

In fact, his utility belt had a phone clip and a flashlight, but nothing of any value should the shit hit the fan.

No taser. No gun. No knife even. The guy hadn't asked his name or for ID.

He drew in a breath as he rolled up the window, not feeling as confident as he had about the security of this location. He'd have to call Chris and Brody when he parked and get their evaluation. They should have gotten here nearly an hour ago. They should have a feel for the risk level.

"Where do I go?" Rick asked once he'd cleared the gate.

"Turn just after that building up there on the right." At Sierra's direction, Rick did as she'd instructed. He crept along until she pointed through the front window. "That's my trailer, up there on the left."

He didn't love how she was so far from the main buildings. Or that she was in a trailer, alone. She'd do better with a dressing room with people around, than isolated in a trailer parked down the road. But what did he know about the workings of a movie lot?

Next to nothing. He sure as hell was going to learn though.

He pulled the truck in front of the trailer and threw the gearshift into park. She had her door open before he had a chance to stop her. He'd put her next to the trailer so his side of the truck was more exposed, but that didn't mean he'd intended her to leap out.

"Dammit." Cussing under his breath, Rick left the keys in the ignition and flung his own door open. He ran around to stand next to her.

The whole way he kept an eye on their surroundings, looking for anything amiss. Again, not that he would know what was usual and what wasn't, which is why he'd wanted her to stay safely in the truck until he'd called Chris.

"Sierra, will you please stop a second and listen to me."

"Did you ask me to do something?" She looked at him over the top of her dark, no doubt designer and overpriced, sunglasses.

"I didn't have a chance to. You didn't give me

even a second."

She lifted one delicate shoulder. "Sorry. I want to drop off my bag and then go for a run."

"Now?"

"Yes. Why not? You said yourself we're here early."

Rick wasn't happy with them even standing out in the open outside her trailer—never mind running all over the lot—until he knew the state of things.

In fact, he'd much prefer if they could hold this conversation inside her trailer—after he made sure it was clear, of course.

If Chris and Brody hadn't gotten to it yet, he'd have to make sure there was no one inside, sweep it for surveillance, check it for explosives. It would have been easier to do that with her locked away safely in his truck.

Obviously annoyed with him, Sierra folded her arms. "You promised we could go for a run today."

"I know I did. Just give me a chance to talk to Chris—" The hair on the back of Rick's neck stood up about the same time he felt the unmistakable whizz of a bullet pass too damn close to his face.

Years of training kicked Rick into action. Without thinking, he'd knocked Sierra to the ground, shielding her with his body.

Sierra hit the ground with a grunt. "Rick. What the hell—"

"Sniper!" His brain worked only slightly slower than his body as he reviewed what had happened seconds before.

"What?" Obviously things had happened so fast, Sierra had missed it. She didn't realize they'd been shot at.

He sure as hell had felt it—the rush of the bullet too close for comfort. The splintering of the fiberglass trailer just behind him where the shot had hit. He'd decide later if it was better she was blissfully ignorant of exactly how close that bullet had come to hitting him, or not.

Judging by the angle of the bullet, the shot would have come from the other side of the street.

Where they were now, on the ground between the truck and Sierra's trailer, put the bulk of his vehicle between them and the shooter. But that would only remain the case if the shooter didn't relocate. The fact was he could very well be on the move.

"Can you get off me now?" Her annoyed muffled request from beneath him proved she still wasn't taking this threat seriously.

What would it take? Her getting actually hit? Him taking a bullet? Both were definitely possibilities given the circumstances.

Keeping that reality in mind, Rick lifted just a bit of his weight off her and said, "We have to go."

"Go where?"

"Away from here. Someplace where people aren't shooting at us." It was the best answer Rick could come up with.

Obviously, the lot wasn't secure. He didn't need to call Chris to confirm that. He did need to tell them what was happening though.

Rick rolled them closer to the truck until they were almost beneath it. He pulled out his cell and punched Chris's number. They'd need to get into the truck eventually but more pressing was the need to call in back up.

As he kept his eyes on their surroundings, he couldn't see Sierra beneath him, but he could feel her breathing hard and fast, probably from anger at him more than fear of the shooter.

Stubborn, hard-headed woman.

He needed her to listen and follow orders otherwise her usual obstinate, loose canon attitude could get them both killed.

Rick punched to dial Chris. After two rings he heard, "Hey. You on your way here?"

"We're here and fucking dodging bullets outside Sierra's trailer."

"What?" Chris's tone rose. "I put you on speaker so Brody can hear. Tell me where you are so I can get to you."

It wasn't as if there were any street signs and he could give them an address. It was a damn movie lot. "I drove in through the front gate, hung a right at the first building on the right. There's a row of trailers up that street. You'll see my truck."

And their dead bodies if Chris and Brody didn't move faster and get here before the sniper got brave and came out of his hide.

"On our way. Hang tight, bro."

Rick reached down and maneuvered his weapon out of the holster beneath his pants leg. The pistol wasn't much of a match for a high-powered sniper rifle with a scope but it was something.

It would work just fine at close range if the bastard was stupid enough to walk around this truck and face Rick head-on, man to man.

Sierra had said that she thought her stalker could be either a male or a female, but Rick had to disagree.

If the threats had been limited to just the photos and a note, a mental battle, an attack of intimidation, maybe he'd buy into the theory it was a woman. But now there was firepower added to the list of assaults.

Call him a chauvinist, but that screamed to him that their opponent in this deadly game wasn't a female.

And speaking of female . . . Sierra was still crushed beneath him breathing hard enough he feared she'd hyperventilate. He felt exactly how small she was. Her build was slight, and she was too damn thin, like too many of Hollywood's darlings were to try and please the overly critical public.

Rick glanced down at her but couldn't see her well enough to determine how upset she was. A fall of hair shielded her face from view.

"You okay?" he asked.

She moved her head in what was half nod, half shake but didn't speak.

Tires squealing had Rick whipping his head up, wishing he had someplace close and safe to stash Sierra so he could do something proactive. Something other than lying there like a slug while playing human shield.

Who the hell knew he should have asked Jon for body armor too? For both of them.

He recognized Brody's truck and breathed freely for the first time in minutes. Finally confident that they'd get out of this situation, he pushed up, taking his weight off Sierra. "My guys are here."

"Now what?"

"Now we get you the hell out of here and someplace safe."

"Where?"

"We'll figure that out as we go."

As a security van squealed onto the scene and Chris and Brody flanked the truck, guns drawn and eyes peeled on anyplace the shooter could be hiding, Rick let Sierra sit up. She leaned against the truck tire with him squatting in front of her so she was still shielded.

She frowned at him, looking angry. "You mean you don't have a plan?"

What the hell? The situation had just changed literally minutes before and she was pissed he didn't have a plan? "Not at the moment, no."

"Then what am I paying you for?"

Rick tempered his own anger, although not completely. He had a few choice words he was weighing, but he considered how angry Jon and Zane would be if he said them to their big client.

Chris backed around the truck and saved Rick from his own tongue and the potential backlash of speaking his mind.

"You a'ight?" Chris's gaze swept Rick and Sierra before he went back to surveying the area.

"Yeah. We're good." Rick figured if Sierra was well enough to bitch, she was doing just fine.

"What's the plan?" Brody rounded the other side of the truck.

Rick heard Sierra's snort at that question and chose to ignore it. "I want her off this lot."

"Agreed." Brody nodded.

"And long term?" Chris asked.

"Out of town until we catch this guy." Obviously the only way to protect her was to remove her from the situation.

He respected her for wanting to keep working, but after today, that wasn't going to happen. Since the damn movie folks couldn't keep the lot secure, they would just have to deal with it.

A security officer came around the truck. "Everyone all right?"

Rick glared through his sunglasses at the man, who still had no weapon to speak of. "Another inch and I'd have a hole in my head God didn't intend me to have. Besides that, yeah, we're okay."

"Jesus." The guard glanced around, pulling his cell off his utility belt. Rick supposed he was calling in reinforcements, who likely would be equally unarmed and unprepared for this situation.

Now, more than ever, Rick missed the teams. Thank God he had back up in the form of Chris and Brody. "Anybody call Jon or Zane?"

"Yeah, I did while Brody was driving us to find you. They should be here any minute, with the police. They were all together in a meeting with the hotel when we called."

Crap. They'd be in the police station for hours filling out reports after this shit. Rick hated reports. That was one thing he didn't miss about the teams.

He drew in a breath and turned his attention back to Sierra. At least she should be safe in the police station. That would give him and the guys time to regroup and figure out their next move.

In the back of his mind Rick knew the shooter would be doing the same thing—planning his next move.

That sealed Rick's determination. He'd do everything in his power to convince everyone that Sierra needed to be kept under lock and key, whether she liked it or not.

Knowing her, she wasn't going to like that one bit.

CHAPTER TWELVE

Sierra drew in a breath as the police officer sitting across the desk from her asked the same question over and over again, just in a slightly different form. "As I told you before, I really didn't see anyone or anything."

She wasn't a suspect, so why did she feel as if she was the one being interrogated?

"Go over the events for me one more time."

"I already did that. Twice."

"Do it one more time, Ms. Cox. Please." His tone remained even and calm.

Good thing he had enough patience for both of them. Sierra was rapidly losing hers.

She sighed. "We drove through the gate of the lot. Rick was behind the wheel. I was in the passenger seat. We were in his truck."

"What kind of truck?"

"I don't know. The kind with an open back

86

thingy. You know, where you put things."

"A pick-up truck?" the officer asked.

"Yes. A big one."

Huge actually. The kind of truck a man drove when he was making up for shortcomings in other areas.

Interesting theory regarding her bodyguard, and it would also explain why Rick was so pushy and bossy. She rubbed her elbow. She'd hit it pretty hard when he'd knocked her to the ground. That was definitely going to leave a bruise.

"Were the windows open?"

"No." She rethought that answer. "Mine was closed but he had rolled his down to talk to the guard at the gate."

"Did he roll his back up?"

"I don't remember." And she really couldn't see what this had to do with anything.

"Okay, then what?"

"He asked me where to go. I told him how to get to my trailer."

"Which was?" he prompted.

"Exactly where you found us when you drove up." What the hell? Was this guy brain damaged or just destined to be annoying?

"I mean what path did you take in the truck."

"We drove past the main building and turned right. The trailer is just past there. On the left. It's maybe a quarter of a mile, I guess." She lifted one shoulder, beyond caring at this point.

How had Rick escaped this inquisition? He wasn't in the room with her. As far as she knew, he was out having a nice meal somewhere with his bruiser friends.

Meanwhile, she was being held in this room like a prisoner with nothing but crappy police station coffee and no food.

God, she was starving. And she'd give anything for a Starbucks sugar-free vanilla latte.

Would they bring her one if she asked?

"Go on." The police officer's prompting knocked her out of her caffeine and food fantasies.

She drew in another loud breath. If the guy couldn't see by now she was annoyed, he was denser than she'd thought.

"I opened the passenger side door of the truck. I stepped down. I closed the door of the truck behind me. I had my bag on my left shoulder. It's a Hermes I bought in Paris. I was wearing my Prada sunglasses. Black ones. I had on the same black yoga pants, zip-up sweatshirt and running shoes I'm wearing now."

Sierra ran through the events, purposefully filling her recount with details she knew were of no consequence to demonstrate to her inquisitor exactly how pointless this questioning was.

He didn't seem to notice. "And where was Mr. Mann?"

"He got out of his side of the truck."

"Which side?" he asked.

"The driver's side since, you know, he was driving." Holy guacamole, was this man that dumb?

"I meant how was the truck positioned in relation to the trailer and the street?"

"Oh." She frowned, picturing the scene. "I was closest to the trailer. His door was on the street side.

He had to walk around the truck to get to me and the trailer."

The officer nodded. "Did you enter the trailer?"

"No. I was about to but I didn't have a chance before he jumped on top of me and knocked me onto the ground."

All six-foot-whatever inches and at least two hundred and fifty pounds of his muscle-bound brutish body had been on top of hers for what seemed like a very long time. She'd never had a man so huge on top of her before.

Her last boyfriend was in good shape, yes, but he'd been an underwear model. He had plenty of muscles, but he kept himself super lean. Too thin, in her opinion. Brad ate less carbs than she did. He kept himself photo shoot ready and she did have to admit, he photographed well.

When Brad's weight had been on top of her, Sierra had barely felt it. He certainly hadn't been built like Rick.

All big and bulky. Hard and bulging. When he was on top of her, she'd been very much aware he was there.

She swallowed hard, refusing to let the brute get to her. He might have the over developed body of Hercules but he had the super-sized attitude to go with it. Always telling her what to do. Pushing her around.

Sure, he'd probably look pretty amazing with his shirt off.

His pants too since she hadn't missed the size of the man's thighs. Holy hell, how did he get those quads so big? But being with a man like him would definitely not be worth dealing with the ego that came with the bod. Nope.

"Ms. Cox?" The officer's voice knocked her out of her internal debate about the pros and cons of sleeping with a man like Rick.

"Um, sorry, did you ask me something?"

"I said we've got enough for now. You're free to go. We'll call if we have any further questions."

"Thank you." Now that she had been set free, she wasn't sure where to go. "Do you know where my manager is?"

"I'm not sure, but the group of men who came in with you were outside in the waiting area last I saw. Mr. Mann said he'd be waiting for you."

No doubt he would be, like any good watchdog. She stood and waited for the officer to open the door for her. "Thanks."

Sierra dug into her bag and pulled out her sunglasses. She'd rather not be recognized coming out of a police station if she could help it. Of course, if word had spread and the paparazzi were outside, no sunglasses would prevent her from being recognized, and photographed, and speculated on.

Sometimes she hated her life. Particularly now, as Rick strode toward her with an expression of determination on his face.

"Come with me."

"Yes, sir." As if she had a choice as he gripped her elbow with one beefy hand and turned her down the hall. "Where are we going? If you don't mind my asking, that is."

Hopefully her sarcasm had penetrated the thick

muscle between his ears.

"You are going to the ladies bathroom." He gave her a little push toward the door.

"I don't have—"

"Just go." He drew in a breath. "Please?"

"Fine." She scowled at being told what to do yet again, but he had said please. She supposed she should reward good behavior.

Sierra pushed through the door and came face to face with a smiling blonde who looked at her like she knew her.

The woman stepped forward. "Hi, I'm Darci Mann. I'm Rick's sister."

"Oh. Um, hi." Surprised that his sister wasn't Amazonian in proportions, Sierra took Darci's offered hand and shook it.

"Rick and Chris have a plan to get you out of here."

"Okay. I guess it involves you?"

"It does." Darci beamed a wide smile at her. She looked much too happy about the whole thing. "I'm sorry. I'm just such a fan. Meeting you in person is huge for me, but to be able to help you and be part of another GAPS assignment—I can't tell you how exciting that is."

Fan girls, Sierra was more than used to. But something else Darci had said, about helping on *another* assignment, was interesting. "You've worked with them before?"

"Only once and if Rick had anything to say about it, I'd never do it again, but this is kind of an emergency situation. They needed me so he couldn't object."

Ah, so Rick ordered his sister around too. Good to know Sierra wasn't the only one in that regard.

"So what's the plan?" Sierra asked.

"I walked in a few minutes ago wearing what's in this bag." Darci thrust a duffle bag forward. "We're close enough in size that the guys figure if you walk out of here, alone, wearing the same clothes I had on, with your hair in a ponytail and the hat and sunglasses, anyone watching won't know it's you."

It might just work—to get her out of the building at least. One question remained. "Then what?"

"My car is parked right outside." Darci held up the keys. "You get in and drive down the block. Turn right at the first light. Rick will be waiting there for you."

"How will he get out of the building without being spotted?"

"He should have already left by now. He and Brody were going to leave here together and hop into Brody's truck. He figures anyone looking will think they ran out for food or whatever. Then they'd wait around to see when you come out."

"But I never will because I'll be already gone." Sierra could see how this plan might just work. "What about you?"

"I'll just walk out. I'm in different clothes that I carried in, inside the bag." Darci pulled the rubber band out of her hair and it cascaded to her shoulders. "No one will think anything of it. I could be an employee who's been inside working for hours. I'm going to take Rick's truck home since you two will have my car for the foreseeable future."

Foreseeable future? "Where are we going?"

"I don't know. Rick wouldn't tell me. As if I would ever tell anyone. Whatever." Darci rolled her eyes.

Sierra had to smile feeling a kinship with this woman who found Rick as frustrating as she did. "Thank you for helping me."

Darci dismissed the thanks with a wave of one hand. "It was nothing. I'm happy to help."

"Seriously. If there's anything I can ever do for you."

The young blonde smiled. "An autograph when you're back and safe would be great."

Sierra laughed. "I can probably do a little better than that but okay, you got it."

Hell, if GAPS actually managed to find this crazy stalker who Rick believed was shooting at her today, she'd get them all tickets for the red carpet for the movie release.

These guys probably looked pretty good in tuxedos—if they could find any that fit. Roger would eat that up.

She smiled at that thought as she moved into one of the stalls to get changed in private in case anyone else came into the bathroom.

CHAPTER THIRTEEN

"What are you doing?"

Sierra glanced up and saw Rick's eyes wide. "I'm checking the posts on my Fan Page on Facebook."

She had to hold on to the door's armrest as Rick hit the breaks and swerved the car onto the shoulder of the highway, bringing it to a stop and rocking Sierra forward.

As he let out a string of curses that might make a less worldly woman blush, she asked, "What's the matter?"

"Your phone's not off?"

"No." She held it up for him to see the display.

More cusses followed as he extended his hand and said, "Give it."

"What? No." Frowning, she pulled the phone away and out of range of his grasp. "And nice language. Do you talk that way to your mother and sister?"

"If either one of them were putting our lives in jeopardy by doing something stupid, yeah, I sure as hell would." His nostrils flared with each fast breath. His eyes looked hard and angry beneath brows that were drawn low.

This guy was more dramatic than she was and she was the one who was an actor. "How is checking Facebook putting our lives in jeopardy?"

He drew in a breath and let it out slowly. "Sierra, there could be a tracker on your phone."

"How would they have gotten access to my phone?"

"How did they get access to the inside of your trailer? And your hotel room?" He cocked up one sandy brow. "And with today's technology, they won't even need access to your device. They can track your location by which cell towers the signal is bouncing off."

Her eyes widened as she wondered if what he said was true.

She stared down at the phone in her hand, seeing it in a whole new light now that it might be a way for someone to spy on her. She was getting pretty tired of having her privacy invaded by whoever this nutcase stalker was.

"So what do I do?"

"Turn it off. Just power it down for now. When we stop somewhere, I'll take it apart. Remove the chip and the battery. Then we'll be certain there's no way anyone can track it."

"Okay." She powered down the phone, to Rick's obvious relief.

"Thank you."

"You're welcome."

The idea of him dismantling her phone wasn't exactly appealing, but there was a newer version out and it came in a new color. She'd been meaning to upgrade anyway. And if he broke it, she'd have something to hold over him until they parted ways, for however long that was.

That raised another question. "Where are we going, anyway?"

"Someplace safe." He checked the side mirror and pulled back onto the highway now that his panic over her cell phone was over.

"You won't even tell me?" Jeez. She knew he hadn't told Darci, but keeping it secret from her seemed really ridiculous. Unless he blindfolded her she'd know where they were.

"Would it make a difference if you knew?" He shot her a sideways glance.

Not really. Rick was behind the wheel speeding somewhere. He was in the driver's seat both literally and figuratively. She had to go with him, a slave to his whim, but that wasn't the point. She wanted to know where they were going.

"Yes, it will make a difference."

"Fine. We're heading for North Carolina."

"North Carolina? Why?"

"Because the Outer Banks is a tourist destination. No one will think twice of a couple of people coming or going, or keeping to themselves. And mostly because we were able to rent a cottage on short notice. Three bedrooms at the beach and only two hundred bucks a night." He grinned at her, looking very smug about his bargain shopping.

"Two hundred a night total? For a three bedroom house at the beach?"

"Yup." He looked singularly pleased with himself. "But don't expect the Taj Mahal. The owner referred to it as a surf shack in the ad."

A shack? The price made much more sense now. She frowned at their destination and what would be her accommodations for the foreseeable future. "Are we on that tight of a budget? Aren't you billing me for all your expenses, including this beach shack?"

"I'm sure Jon is, but accounting isn't my department. We're going there because no one would expect Sierra Cox to be staying in an inexpensive cottage on Ocracoke Island."

"No doubt. And that's a terrible name, by the way. Ocracoke."

Brow cocked, he shot her a sideways glance. "I'll be sure to inform the chamber of commerce when we arrive."

"Is it beach front, at least?"

"Yes, princess. It is beach front." He rolled his eyes.

"Don't call me princess."

"Don't act like one and I won't." He didn't even bother glancing her direction as he issued that directive.

She didn't have a suitable retort so she chose the silent treatment.

That plan worked for about five miles of highway, before she had more questions. Holding them in until he talked first became impossible.

Finally, Sierra asked, "Does Roger know where we're going?"

"No."

"No? Why not?"

"We don't know who to trust right now."

"Not even Roger? Are you crazy? You really think he had anything to do with those photos or the bug in my room?"

"I don't know. He certainly had access."

"Okay, even if he did, you can't believe he took a shot at you today. If anyone actually did shoot at you at all."

"You don't believe me?" His eyes widened as he turned to glare at her.

"Keep your eyes on the road, please."

"I know how to multitask. And I damn well know when a bullet comes within an inch of my face. Don't have any doubt about that. I've been shot at enough."

She would have asked how and why he'd been shot at so much, but she was too flabbergasted he suspected her manager. Her closest friend. And the nearest person she had to family for years now.

"No. I won't believe it's Roger."

"That's fine. You don't have to. We're still playing this cautiously. He's been told you're safe but there's no need for him to know where you are. Until we catch this guy, and as long as I'm in charge, we're not taking any chances."

It must be a very nerve wracking existence to live in a constant state of paranoia. Sierra didn't trust many people, other than Roger, but she didn't actively go around distrusting everyone either.

Unlike Mr. Tough guy here.

"Do you trust anyone at all?" she asked.

"Yes."

Sierra didn't believe him. She twisted in her seat so she could face him without turning her neck. "Oh really? Who?"

"My teammates. Every one of them would kill or die for me."

That was certainly a dramatic statement. "You say that but you don't know that for sure."

He leveled a stare at her. "Yes, I do."

The low, ominous tone in his voice and the flat stare of his eyes had her feeling uncomfortable. Who the hell were these guys?

"Sorry. I didn't mean to offend you."

"You didn't. It's just the way things are. I know they have my six no matter what. Even guys you don't like very much you'd do anything to protect and you trust them to do the same for you." He shrugged. "And then there's my sister. I trust her."

Sierra let out a burst of air. "Now I know you're lying. You wouldn't even tell her where we were going."

He shot her a sideways glance. "I'd trust her with my life, not with yours. There's a difference. And besides, it's safer if she doesn't know where we are. Someone is after you, and I'm not sure they'd stop at hurting others to get to you. Yes, Darci drives me nuts most days, but we're family. I know when push came to shove she'd be there for me. You can always trust blood."

No, you can't. She knew that very well. She'd paid the price, in money and a piece of her soul.

"I don't have anyone like that."

"What? No family?" He glanced at her.

She snorted. "Family, yes. Family I trust. No."

Not as far as she could throw them.

"Well, I'm sorry for that. That's a sad way to live."

She bristled at his pity and settled into an unhappy silence, until Rick reached into his pocket and pulled out a cell phone.

After he had yelled at her about her cell, he had one of his own?

Rick answered the call. "Hey, what's the sit rep?"

Sierra watched open mouthed. "You have a phone?"

When Rick shushed her and continued with his phone conversation, she nearly crawled out of her skin. Waiting for him to hang up only served to ramp up her already high blood pressure.

Of all the gall. To lecture her about her cell. Make her power it off. Tell her he was going to dismantle her six hundred dollar phone. And he was talking on his?

"Yes, princess? You were saying."

She grit her teeth. He was provoking her. He didn't need to. She was already ready to boil over. "You have a cell phone?"

"Burner phones. Brand new. Untraceable. Jon bought one for him, Chris and me on his way to the police station."

She eyed the phone in his hand critically. He could tell her anything. How would she know if it was true or not?

"I want one too."

He lifted a brow. "Why? Who are you gonna call?"

"I don't know."

"The only way it stays untraceable is if you don't call anyone's phone that could be monitored. If we weren't together, then yes, I'd get you one that you could use just to call me. But I have no intention of leaving your side for the near future. And if I have to leave to go back to my job, Chris is taking over."

She rolled her eyes. "And after Chris, is it Jon's turn? Or Zane's? And wait, what job? Isn't this your job?"

What else could he be full-time if this was only part-time?

"This isn't my only job. No. Just one of them. We aren't all earning six million a year, you know." He shot her a cocky look that told her he'd seen in the media how much she'd signed for on her next movie and he thought it was ridiculous, before he continued, "And Jon and Zane will be leaving for Africa shortly, so Chris and I will be covering the schedule until whenever the bosses are back in country."

Africa? What the hell would they be doing there? Protecting the rhinos?

Confused as each tidbit of information he provided only raised more questions, Sierra shook her head and stared at his profile. This man had more secrets hidden inside his goofy but hot exterior than she'd ever imagined. "Who the hell are you GAPS people?"

He spared her one glance before looking back at

the highway that stretched in front of them. "We're the guys who are gonna keep you alive."

CHAPTER FOURTEEN

"We need to stop."

Sierra's request had Rick glancing at the time displayed on the car's radio.

If he'd figured the trip correctly, they were almost to the ferry that would take them to Ocracoke and the rental house.

His calculations should be pretty accurate. He'd kept the cruise control set for most of the trip so he wouldn't be tempted to drive too much over the speed limit and get pulled over. He couldn't risk having a cop stop them for speeding and recognizing Sierra.

News of her whereabouts would spread like wildfire. Thanks to social media, the gossip mongers didn't need to wait for the next supermarket tabloid to go to print to spread their so-called news. All it took was a cell phone camera and a social media account.

The trip had gone smoothly so far. Only now as they neared the ferry launch had they begun to hit traffic.

The congestion on the road in Hatteras had slowed them down a bit, but they still were close enough to their destination, he didn't want to stop.

He glanced at her. "Can you wait?"

She lifted a brow. "I'm thirsty and I'd like to use the restroom, if you don't mind. There are places all along here for us to stop. Why should I wait?"

Because he'd asked her nicely to didn't seem like a good enough answer. "First off, I don't want you being recognized. If you're thirsty, there's bottled water in the bag on the back seat. If you can wait for a bathroom, we'll be getting out of the car shortly."

She frowned at him. "How shortly?"

"Ten minutes."

"Really?"

"Yes, really."

"Fine." Sierra swiveled her head to stare out the side window.

Figuring her silence was better than her bitching he counted himself lucky and focused on watching for the turn off. He spotted it and flipped on the blinker.

After slowing and making the turn, he pulled up to the line of cars waiting to get on the free ferry onto Ocracoke Island.

He threw the car into park but left the engine idling. For some reason, that move had Sierra scowling at him again.

"Now what are we doing? You said we were

almost there."

"I said we could get out of the car shortly. Not that we'd be at the rental."

She eyed the line of mostly empty cars in front of them and the shops nearby. "Why are we stopped here? What are we waiting for?"

"The ferry. Ocracoke is an island. There are two ways on and off and that's by air or by boat." It was one of the reasons this spot had appealed to Rick. She still didn't look happy so he elaborated. "They run every half hour. We'll be loading in probably twenty minutes or so.

She drew in a big breath and then let it out. "Fine. But I'm getting out of this damn car while we wait."

"Sierra—"

"I'm. Getting. Out." She glared at him, reinforcing the intent behind her staccato words, as if he could have had any doubt.

There was no way he was letting her wander around alone.

"We're both getting out. Just please put the baseball hat on again first."

They had time before they had to be back to the car ten minutes before departure to load the cars onto the ferry. Drivers were allowed to get their spot in line and then leave their vehicles, as long as they were back when they started loading.

Rick knew both the ferry schedule and rules. Just like he would have done before any op while he was in the teams, he had done his research before they'd left. He'd learned as much as he could about the destination and how to get there.

The only difference was that he'd been researching the best access to a beach getaway, rather than to a terrorist stronghold. The location and nature of his assignments had changed but not his dedication to completing them to the best of his ability.

People were already out of their cars and wandering around on the sidewalk, popping into the nearby shops and the food stands by the ferry terminal.

Just ahead was a breathtaking view of the water that Sierra didn't seem to notice. Obviously she wasn't going to admit that if they did have to hide until the threat was resolved this was a pretty damn nice place to do it.

Rick, however, drew in the beauty with an appreciation he knew someone like Sierra could never understand. He'd been forced to bide his time in a lot of places, and this was definitely one of the better ones.

Hell, if Ocracoke had been good enough for Blackbeard to hide out, then it was good enough for them.

Sierra blowing out a breath caught his attention. He looked over to see her pull on the baseball hat Darci had loaned her.

She tugged it low over her brow until it touched her oversized sunglasses in front and reached her low ponytail in back. She flipped down the car's visor and evaluated her reflection in the small mirror there.

"Oh, yeah, no one will recognize me now. Not with this clever disguise." Her sarcasm was clear.

"Which is exactly why I'd rather have you stay inside the car but I know you want out, so we'll get out." Rick was smart enough to choose his battles.

He was willing to let her out of the car for a few minutes, but he also intended to lead her directly to the bathroom and then back.

"I think you just like telling me what to do." Sierra had mumbled the complaint, but he heard it.

Unlike some of the old timers he knew who'd lost the acuteness of their hearing from years in the military around noisy machines and gunfire, Rick's hearing was perfect.

"Eh, ordering you around is just a bonus." He grinned as she huffed before turning to yank open the passenger door.

He was ready for her quick exit this time. He'd already cut the engine and had the keys out of the ignition. He was out of his door and around to the other side before she had a chance to slam her door.

Rick clicked the locks shut and offered her his arm. "Shall we?"

She looked down at the elbow he'd extended to her. "What are you doing?"

"We're undercover, remember? Now take my arm and pretend we're a happy couple."

"Pfft. Good thing pretending is my job."

"Yup. Think of it as just another role." Only this one wasn't for an Academy Award. The stakes were much higher. He figured he'd better warn her of that. "Don't talk to anyone. Not in the ladies room. Not in passing."

"Why not?"

"Your voice is recognizable." And he didn't trust

her to be able to lie on the fly. Acting was one thing. Lying was another. She might be skilled at the former, but he'd been trained by the best in the fine art of the latter.

Rick chose to take Sierra's quick expulsion of breath as her agreement to his request. "Also—"

"Oh, for God's sake, what now?"

"If you want something to eat or drink, let me know and I'll order it and pay. Just like we can't use your cell, we can't use any credit cards. Cash only for everything. Got it?"

"So you're going to be my sugar daddy and pay for me?"

If that was how she wanted to play this role that was fine with him. "Yup."

"Until I get the bill when this is over." The corner of her mouth quirked up in what was almost a smile.

"Exactly." He grinned.

She was loosening up a little if she was joking around with him. That was both good and bad. He didn't need her letting her guard down and getting too complacent, but damn it would be nice if she wasn't going to act like a witch the whole time they'd be cloistered away with only each other for company.

"Fine. But can I go to the bathroom before we start our charade?"

"Sure." As he watched her push through the restroom door, he couldn't help but notice how she filled out his sister's white pants damn nicely.

That was a disturbing thought on so many levels.

He let out a sigh. If circumstances were different,

if this wasn't a job and there wasn't a maniac wielding a sniper rifle after her, he might really enjoy being trapped alone on an island with Sierra Cox.

Running in the waves. Watching the saltwater bead off her skin. Peeling off her wet bikini.

Damn. That would be one hell of a good time—

The door swung wide again and she pranced out, making a beeline for the nearest food stand. She stopped and turned, planting one hand on her hip. "Why are you just standing there? Come on. I'm thirsty. I should probably eat too because God only knows what you'll feed me when we get to this shack you rented."

Or maybe not.

CHAPTER FIFTEEN

Shack was an apt description for the A-line building Sierra currently stood in front of. The one Rick had generously referred to as a beach cottage.

Behind her, Rick sighed deeply. "What? Not good enough for you, princess?"

"I asked you to stop calling me that."

"And I told you I would, as soon as you stopped acting like one. What's wrong with the house?"

"It's . . ." So many adjectives careened through her head it was hard to choose just one.

"Not a mansion? Doesn't have gold plated doorknobs? What?"

She cocked up one brow. "Don't you take an attitude with me."

"No attitude here. I'm just the one trying to keep you alive . . ." He carried in a big canvas duffle bag that looked packed full and heavy.

A bag that big should have wheels. Anyone who

traveled as much as she did knew that. Rick's bag didn't have wheels, proving he wasn't the sharpest tool in the shed even if he did like to pretend he read Sun Tzu.

He dropped the bag on the doorstep and stooped to lift the mat. Emerging with a key, he proceeded to unlock the front door.

"You're kidding me, right? This is your secure hide out? With the front door key under the mat?"

"It will be secure enough once I'm in there." He tipped his head toward the building. "Come on. I can't sweep the house and keep an eye on you out in the front yard at the same time."

Scowling, she begrudgingly followed him through the doorway.

He dumped the bag on the floor and closed the door behind her. "Stay right here. Don't move until I say."

Sierra rolled her eyes. "You should have just brought a guard dog with you."

"If one had been available on short notice, I would have. A bomb sniffing dog would have been even better."

Bomb? He was worried about someone trying to blow her up?

She was still having trouble believing the threat was really as bad as he said.

Having an obsessed fan who pushed the line of what was appropriate with a video camera she could believe. But having one who wanted her dead? That she couldn't wrap her head around.

Rick kneeled on the floor and opened the duffle. Finally, Sierra got a look at what was making it so heavy. It looked as if he'd raided a gun store. Who knows? Maybe he had. She wouldn't be surprised by anything this man did anymore.

He slipped a holster over his arms and shoved a pistol into it. He'd apparently upgraded from just the leg holster.

Next he pulled out the device his friends had brought to her hotel room that morning.

God, had it really been only that morning they'd discovered the camera in the bathroom? So much had happened since then it felt like a lifetime ago.

"I'm going to check the first floor. Stay here." He pinned her with his tough guy glare.

Sierra delivered a salute in response to Rick's order. "Yes, sir."

The corner of his mouth quirked up before he reached out and adjusted the angle of the hand she held over her right brow. "It's more like this. I'll be right back."

She watched as he made his way to the back of the house and into a kitchen area divided from the living room by an island. Glancing down, she evaluated his duffle bag and its contents one more time and drew in a breath.

What was she supposed to do for clothes or other basic necessities like a toothbrush? It was pretty obvious Rick's packing had consisted of raiding some armory somewhere.

Roger might have been right when he said it was likely GAPS was staffed by former military. These guys probably had all served in some branch of service, at least for a couple of years. Long enough to get the scary gun-toting dude look down pat.

Rick reappeared in the room, interrupting her ponderings. "First floor is clear."

"Oh, well, thank God for that." She rolled her eyes at the ridiculousness of his search for bugs or bombs or whatever else.

She doubted her stalker's reach extended to a shack they'd rented only hours prior, located on an island accessible only by boat.

He ignored her sarcasm and headed toward the staircase. "I'm going upstairs. "Don't—"

"Don't move. I know. I got it." She made sure the fact she was humoring him while mocking him was apparent in her tone.

She did, however, resist the urge to remind him that any bad guy could easily bust through the front door and grab her from the very spot he'd ordered her to remain.

He was already up the staircase so he wouldn't have heard anyway. The man's legs were so damn long, he took the stairs two at a time.

Rick was back again in a moment. "Clear."

She rolled her eyes again. "Of course, it was. Hey, do you think there's a nail place on the island? I need a mani/pedi."

He lifted his brows high. "You're not going out for a mani/pedi."

"But—"

"No. I'll paint your damn nails if you need but no going out."

"What? Are you crazy?"

"I've done it before."

"Why? You a cross-dresser?" Given the size of him, that was a ridiculous image.

"No. I used to build models when I was younger. Painting is painting. Doesn't matter if it's the fine detail work on the 1965 Cobra, or your little piggies. I used to polish my high school girlfriend's toes all the time."

This day just got weirder as time passed. "Never mind. I'll survive."

"Good. I'm getting the rest of the stuff out of the car."

"There's more stuff?"

"Yeah. A cooler full of food so we don't have to go out and your suitcase and carry-on."

Her eyes widened. "My suitcase? How did you get that? When?"

"We were already packing you up to move to another hotel. Jon brought your stuff over while you were being questioned at the police station. Same time I stocked up on food."

That made sense but one thing didn't. "When did you, you know, arm up?"

"Arm up? Where'd you get that term from? Some script?" He lifted his brows high. When she scowled at him all he did was laugh. "Darci brought me my things from home."

"You have all that . . . *stuff* lying around your house?" She eyed the bag of weaponry.

"Not lying around. In a secure gun safe with a lock. I gave Darci the combination." He paused, keeping his focus on her. "You have a problem with guns?"

"No. I was just wondering."

"Good." He drew in a breath and looked around. "It's not so bad here you know."

114

"No? It looks like the furniture is from 1979." She hadn't lived through the seventies but she'd seen enough TV shows and movies set then to know this place fit the bill for that era.

"So, things are a little dated. It's neat and it's clean. Even the bathrooms and kitchen look immaculate."

So he hadn't been just looking for bugs of the surveillance nature. Rick had evaluated the cleanliness of his prized rental as well. Probably so she wouldn't complain.

There was still plenty she could find to be unhappy with. The sofa cushions, in a putrid nubby avocado green fabric, looked like they'd been stuffed with lumpy potatoes. She could only imagine what the mattresses looked like.

She looked up in time to see Rick shaking his head at her. "Get used to the place, princess. I'm going to the car to get our stuff."

"Fine."

Little did he know she would have offered to help, at least with her own suitcase. But he'd ordered her to stay put, so she was staying put. That would teach him a lesson to not be such a tyrant.

While he struggled with whatever was hidden away in the car, Sierra decided to see for herself what horrors her accommodations held. She'd only gone a few steps toward the kitchen before a wall of windows faced her. Beyond the salt-frosted glass an endless vista of water stretched, blue and sparkling beneath the rays of the sun.

"Not so bad now, huh?" Rick had somehow snuck up on her.

She turned away from the view. "It is beach front. Just like you said."

He held a large cooler, which he set heavily onto the long wooden table that was in front of the window. Sierra wasn't sure she was up for what he'd brought for them to eat. Probably beef jerky or some other manly treat.

To her surprise, he pulled out a carton of eggs and one of milk, bacon, lettuce, deli packages of cold cuts and some really big steaks. He glanced up and caught her watching him. "There's a couple of grocery bags still in the car with bread, mayo, mustard, salad dressing, potatoes, bottled water and some cans of soup."

"Okay."

He paused with the steak package in his hand. "You're not a vegetarian, are you?"

"No." It was a good thing too, given the amount of meat he'd brought.

"I figure we're set for the next few days, at least."

"Sure. I mean, why would we ever want to leave?"

"Sierra, why aren't you taking this seriously?"

"Because I don't believe this threat is as bad as you think it is."

He closed the refrigerator door and flipped the lid of the cooler shut. But he didn't look happy his cold groceries were all stowed. Instead he shook his head. "I don't believe you're this complacent. How can you possibly be as unconcerned as you're pretending? You're lying. If not to me, than to yourself."

"I'm not lying. Yes, I'm horrified about the camera in my bathroom. The thought of it makes my skin crawl. But an over-the-top fan or some greedy paparazzi trying to sell pictures to the tabloids doesn't mean my life is in danger."

"Sierra, someone either shot at you or they were aiming at me because I was getting between them and you. Either way, it's not good.

She screwed her face up at his theory. "How do you even know it was a bullet?

His eyes popped wide. "I felt the breeze from it flying by my head."

"Maybe it was a big bug or something." She shrugged.

Just when she thought he couldn't look more shocked, his eyes popped wider. "It splintered the doorframe. I had the debris in my hair. Why can't you get it?"

His tone, his treating her like a liar or like she was stupid, had her anger rising.

"Well, maybe if you didn't keep me in the dark about everything, I would get it. I can't use my phone. I can't talk to Roger. I have no clue what kind of investigation is happening. You didn't even want to tell me where we were going."

"Fine. If that's your problem, that you don't know what's going on, I'll tell you. What do you want to know?" He folded his arms over his chest and leaned back against the kitchen table.

"Everything."

He rolled his eyes. "All right. Fine. Ask."

She felt justified in being suspicious of his offer. "So I can ask anything and you'll answer it?

"Yes." He was getting annoyed. Good. She liked that she could get to him like he got to her.

Sierra decided to put this new transparency of his to the test. "Is your family really as sickeningly sweet and happy and normal as you make out or are you full of shit?"

His brows rose high. "I tell you to ask anything and I'll answer and that's what you want to know? About my childhood and family?"

"That and about a dozen other things. But let's start with that."

He shook his head. "How about we'll get to that. First, you need to understand how serious this threat is."

She wasn't in the mood for a lecture and just as she expected, he wasn't willing to answer anything. "I know exactly how serious it is." And it wasn't as bad as he thought. At least, she wouldn't allow herself to believe it was.

Spinning on the rubber sole of her running shoes, she turned and decided to go upstairs.

She'd see what was upstairs. First, because it was away from him. Mostly that actually, but she also had to find herself a bedroom that she might have a hope of getting some sleep in.

And once she found it, she'd slam the door on Rick and his lecture—if this hippy surfer's shack even had doors on the bedrooms.

Stomping to make her displeasure with him known, she ascended the stairs. At the top, there was one larger room and two smaller ones. There was no question which one she was taking.

She was about to go inside and inspect further

when she heard Rick's heavy footsteps on the stairs behind her.

Of course he'd follow her. Not a surprise at all—

The feel of his hand on her arm had her squealing as he spun her to face him.

"Where is your phone?" His eyes flashed.

He looked so angry, she bit back the smart ass reply that had been on the tip of her tongue and instead said, "Downstairs in my purse."

Rick stomped down the stairs. She followed and made it down in time to see him upend her bag and all of her things cascade onto the tabletop.

"What are you doing?"

He pawed through the items on the table, latching on to her cell. He held it up, sneering. "I could ask you the same question, princess. What the hell are you doing posting pictures online?"

"I didn't."

"According to Chris you did. He just texted. Darci saw a new post from you on Instagram. Something about your new shoes. When the fuck are you going to believe me you're in danger? Turning on that phone for even a minute could lead them right to—"

Fuming, Sierra took a step closer. He was big but she was mad.

"I didn't turn my phone on. I didn't post anything. I'm not even wearing shoes. You ass."

"Then how—"

"I have a social media intern. She posts as me. All the time. All sorts of things. When would I have posted? I've been with you the entire time. You obnoxious, mean, nasty . . . caveman."

She delivered a slap to his arm, hard enough it stung her hand. He probably didn't even feel it. His damn muscles were like iron. She turned away so he wouldn't see the angry tears in her eyes.

This time, his hand on her arm was gentle. "Sierra."

"What?" She had no intention of turning around, but he turned her toward him.

"I'm sorry. I shouldn't have assumed."

"You're right. You shouldn't have." Her emotions all over the place, she teetered on the precipice between anger and tears.

The tears won out. As one big fat one spilled onto her cheek, she slapped at him again, hitting his chest this time. His damn pec muscle was as hard as the rest of him.

She cradled her hand against her chest. "Ow."

The corners of his lips tipped up. "You done hitting me now?"

"Yes."

"Come here." Rick pulled her to him. "I knew you were bound to break soon. It's too much stress to hold in."

"I'm not crying from the stress. I'm crying because I'm so mad at you." She pulled her head away from his chest to glare at him.

"That's fine. I'm pretty tough skinned. I can handle it." His gaze dropped to her lips, before he pulled it back up to her eyes. He brushed his thumb across the wet skin where the tear had run down her cheek.

It had been so long since a man had touched her for real. Her last relationship had ended long ago.

The only physical contact she'd had since had been in front of the cameras and crew.

She drew in a shaky breath. She wasn't sure if that was from everything happening with the stalker or the fact Rick was making her feel things inside she hadn't felt in a long time.

It was ridiculous. She'd thought she'd hated him. Or at least she hated how he acted.

She shouldn't be so aware of the heat of his skin against hers. His casual touch shouldn't make her stomach tighten. And she really shouldn't be picturing him tossing her onto that bed upstairs.

"Rick?"

"Yeah?"

"Don't get the wrong idea. I'm still pissed at you. This doesn't mean anything."

"What doesn't—" Before Rick could finish whatever he'd been about to say, Sierra fisted his shirt and pulled, bringing his mouth close enough she could crash her lips against his.

He drew in a deep breath through his nose and leaned into the kiss. She felt the breadth of his hands span her hips as he pulled her closer.

Angling his head, he took the kiss deeper.

His mouth was warm. His body against hers reminded her of all she'd been missing during her extended period of self-imposed celibacy.

A moan she never intended, one of mingled frustration and satisfaction, snuck out of her. He responded with a deep grumbling groan of his own and kissed her harder.

He slid one leg between hers, settling in as if he was going to stay awhile. Which had her thinking—

why hadn't he pulled away from her? He should be telling her they needed to remain vigilant in case they were followed. He should be setting up cameras or cleaning his guns or something.

What kind of professional was he? He shouldn't be fraternizing with the clients. What would the owners of GAPS think of this behavior?

Sierra pulled back from the kiss. "Why are you kissing me?"

Frowning, he leaned back, but he didn't move his hands. "Because you kissed me."

She tried to ignore the feel of those big fingers pressing into her flesh. "Yes, but why aren't you fighting me on it?"

The furrow between his brows disappeared as his lips tipped up in a smile. "Hey, I'm up for hate sex as much as the next guy. What's the matter, princess? Who are you trying to talk out of this? You or me?"

She narrowed her eyes. "You know I hate when you call me that."

"I know. That's why I did it." Rick's crooked smile didn't last long before his mouth was on hers again. He kissed her hard and then pulled back. "Make up your mind yet?"

She had to swallow the dryness from her throat to be able to talk. "About what?"

"If I'm going to take you upstairs or go make myself a sandwich instead."

She felt her brow furrow. "That's the choices?"

"Yeah."

"And you're saying you'd be just fine if I said go make a sandwich?"

"Sure. I'm hungry and the store had the really good turkey breast, not that fake stuff." He brushed one thumb over her forehead. "Stop frowning. You'll get wrinkles. That'll probably cost you a good million a film."

His cocky grin as he poked fun at her didn't match the physical evidence, the hard length pressing into her as he went back to holding her hips tightly against him.

He might pretend to be immune to the temptation she'd dangled before him. He could say he'd be just as happy with a cold turkey sandwich, but he was lying. His body told the truth.

Rick went from just holding her, to making small circles with his thumbs. His hands were so huge he could reach all the way around to her stomach.

That lazy motion against the thin, skin-tight fabric of the exercise pants did things to her. Made her want his hands in other places. She was breathing heavier. Her pulse pounded.

Her damn body was betraying her by craving the enemy's touch. She was obviously as into hate sex as Rick.

Fine. As long as they both knew where they stood, there was no problem.

"You can make your sandwich later."

"All right." His voice was low and throaty, his eyes narrow as his heavily-lidded gaze met hers.

He dropped his hold on her and just when she thought he'd toss her over his shoulder like the caveman he was, and carry her up the stairs to have hot, angry sex with her, he turned toward the door.

Bending down, he grabbed the strap of the duffle

and hoisted it onto his shoulder before turning back to her.

So much for the big prelude she'd worked up in her imagination. The man had as much of a hard-on for his weapons as he did for her.

He was so annoying. And frustrating. And . . .

Damn, she was totally willing to overlook all of that. At least for the next hour or so.

CHAPTER SIXTEEN

Duffle bag on his shoulder, Rick swept his arm toward the staircase. "Ladies first."

She let out an unhappy sounding *humph.* Why, he didn't know.

What? Had she expected him to sweep her off her feet and carry her up the damn stairs?

He had a bag full of guns and ammo as well as sophisticated equipment. He wasn't leaving all that out in the open downstairs while he was upstairs getting busy with the lovely but annoying Sierra Cox.

He watched her ahead of him on the staircase. That little wiggle that came with every step she took was enough to make him be able to ignore she was still wearing his sister's pants. He'd remedy that concern immediately by stripping the spirited Ms. Cox of that outfit and tossing her onto the mattress.

Inside the largest bedroom in the three bedroom

cottage, which no doubt Sierra planned to claim as her own, Rick slid the duffle bag off his shoulder and set it onto the floor.

Sierra was still moving toward the bed when he caught up with her. He reached out and spun her toward him. She was so tiny in the midsection he could practically wrap his hands completely around her waist.

He pulled her close, catching her gaze with his. "I'm going to feed you while we're here and you're going to eat."

"We're standing next to the bed and you're still thinking about food." She let out a *humph*. "That figures."

"Don't worry. I can think about two things at once."

One dark brow rose. "I'm not so sure about that."

Rick smiled, shaking his head. "You are such a brat."

Brat hadn't been the B-word he had in mind, but he'd tempered himself.

She obviously wanted a good old-fashioned hate fuck and he was just the man to give it to her. But Sierra Cox was as changeable as the wind and one wrong word could change her mind. Send her into a tailspin that ended with him on the wrong side of the bedroom door.

Before she could respond he kissed her hard.

Kissing Sierra was one way to make sure she kept her comments to herself. Rick had another way to occupy her mouth that he'd get to later.

That plan had him throbbing inside his pants.

For now, he was happy to take her mouth, hard

and demanding, just as he intended to treat the rest of her. Just like he knew she wanted.

She made that desire apparent when she yanked hard, pulling his shirt out from where it had been tucked into his waistband.

After running her hands up the bare skin of his back, she raked her nails back down hard enough her fingers left a painful tingle behind. Possibly not hard enough to draw blood, but probably hard enough to leave scratch marks.

Marking her territory? Or just trying to show him who was boss?

Probably the latter, since she wouldn't want him for more than a night or two. She was scratching an itch. He knew that.

That was okay with him. He had a few itches to scratch himself.

Sierra pulled her head back. "Take off this damn thing." She slapped at his shoulder holster.

Rick took a step back and went to work on ridding himself of both the shoulder and the leg holster. "Gladly. You take off my sister's clothes."

"Why? You having problems down below because I'm wearing your sister's clothes?" As she got an evil glint in her eye, the term she-devil came to mind.

"I have no problems *down below*. I promise you that." And he'd show her as soon as he had rid himself of his weapons.

He slid the shoulder holster off and made short work of pulling off his shirt. He tossed it onto the only chair in the room and turned back to find Sierra's stare focused on him. She could look all she wanted, as long as she continued to undress while she did it.

So far, she'd only gotten as far as her sneakers and socks as she sat on the edge of the mattress.

He'd have to help her, as soon as he completed the mission of getting himself stripped first.

Rick had a leg holster to deal with and still he beat Sierra in the unofficial race to get naked. She had taken an inordinate amount of time to unzip his sister's hoodie and she still had her T-shirt and pants to take off. Not to mention whatever treats of the lingerie variety awaited him beneath.

In nothing but his briefs, Rick strode to where Sierra stood next to the bed. He'd finish what she'd started, and in far less time than she would on her own.

"Come here. Let me do it." Reaching out, he grabbed the bottom of her shirt and pulled it over her head. Tossing that aside, he moved in for her pants next. One yank had those down around her ankles.

He lifted her by the waist and easily tossed her onto the bed. She landed with a bounce as he tugged the pants off her feet. He took quick note of her pretty pink painted toenails before he moved his attention to more important things—the panties that topped her long, slender legs.

A part of Rick's subconscious mind remained braced for her mood to change one more time, as it did so easily and often over the short time he'd known her.

That it had been such a short time made it even more insane she'd kissed him and led him up to bed. He could see she hadn't changed her mind yet. She looked up at him from beneath heavy lids while she watched him slide his hands up her thighs toward his end goal.

Rick slid his fingers over her underwear. The fabric was as smooth and soft against his fingertips as her skin had been.

The damn things probably cost easily ten times what he spent on his underwear. He didn't want to risk upsetting her should he accidently tear them, so he took his time pulling the delicate panties down her legs.

While kneeling on the bed, he tossed them to the chair with the rest of their clothes. He turned back to her, leaning low, moving over her.

She watched him until he slid his hands up between those silky thighs of hers, all the way to a spot that had her closing those eyes that had been focused on him.

Pressing her head back into the pillow, she hissed in a breath.

Another brush of his thumb elicited a sexy as hell sound from her. It was worlds better than the usual complaints that came out of her mouth.

This encounter wasn't going as he'd planned—it was far better.

He'd half expected her to be giving him orders throughout the whole damn time he was in bed with her. Like he was some servant paid to please her. She was paying him, but not for this.

She reacted to his every touch. Without comment. Without censure. Without criticism.

Using sex to tame this sharp-tongued shrew he

couldn't help wanting in spite of it all was an intriguing concept, and proving to be a definite possibility.

She was boneless, putty beneath his hands as he spread her legs and lowered his head. When his mouth replaced his fingers, Sierra gasped, lifting her hips, pressing more closely against his tongue.

In minutes, she was trembling beneath his hands.

His own need ramped up in direct relation to her pleasure. He worked her harder until her cries bounced off the ceiling and walls.

He wasted no time pulling himself up her body and plunging inside her wet heat. Her muscles convulsed around him with aftershocks from the orgasm.

As Rick lost himself in the feel of her, it was easy to forget who she was. What she was.

Right now, they weren't spoiled star and hired protection. They were just a man and woman, taking exactly what they needed from each other.

He had no idea if it was two minutes or twenty-two, but he was winded and sweating when Sierra raked her nails down his back and clutched his ass, holding him deep.

That was all it took for him to lose hold of the control he'd somehow managed to maintain. He careened over the edge just as she did.

He'd just rolled off her when she turned her head on the pillow.

She frowned. "You're a dick, you know that?"

He opened his eyes wide. "Excuse me?"

She hadn't even caught her breath yet, neither had he, and she was already cussing at him. Over what, he couldn't even imagine. She seemed to have as good a time as he did.

"You didn't even ask me if it was okay if you could . . . you know. Do that. Finish. Inside me."

Rick lifted a brow. She had no problem yelling at him seconds after he'd been inside her, but she couldn't say *that* word. He would have laughed at that if he didn't think it would throw her over the deep end and into a tizzy she might never come back from.

"I didn't have to ask. I saw your birth control pills." Besides, being shy was not one of Sierra's traits. He had no doubt she would have had no problem telling him if it wasn't safe.

Her eyes widened. "You went through my stuff?"

"No, they were right out in the open next to the sink in the bathroom at the hotel." When she didn't look satisfied, he continued, "Remember, when I was finding the camera and saving you from being spied on?"

That seemed to take a bit of the wind out of her pending rant. "Well, I don't have those pills now, do I?"

"Yes, you do have them. Remember? I got your stuff. As soon as I get the suitcase out of the trunk you'll have everything." He waited and when she didn't say more he rolled back on top of her. Bracketing her head between his forearms, Rick stared into her eyes. "Anything else you got to bitch about, princess?"

"You're an ass." She pursed her lips together, her eyes narrowed in anger.

This time he did smile. "There's the Sierra I know and love. Now, let's go for that hate sex you wanted so badly one more time."

Though he was sure she had plenty to say, he didn't give her time before he slammed his mouth against hers.

She didn't try and stop him. He knew she wouldn't. Sparring—verbal, physical, it didn't matter—obviously got her turned on.

Her tongue wrestled with his as he slid inside her, taking possession of both her mouth and her body.

Her fingernails dug into him again. He'd have marks all over him from her but he supposed he should expect nothing less. A man couldn't tangle with a hellcat like Sierra Cox and not walk away with a few battle scars to show for it.

She broke the kiss and bit his chest, her teeth latching onto his skin hard enough she'd surely leave behind a bruise.

A bolt of mingled pain and pleasure shot straight through him. He hissed in a breath and let it out with a groan.

Oh, yeah. He got off from the battle of wills and flesh just as much as she did.

He'd definitely make sure to piss her off again later. Hopefully, quite a few more times before this siege was over.

CHAPTER SEVENTEEN

It seemed that one moment Sierra was beneath Rick, his bulk blocking the sun streaming through the window, and the next thing she knew she was opening her eyes to a dark room, all alone in the bed.

There was a scratchy wool blanket tossed over her naked body. She didn't remember pulling it over herself. He must have done it, which was far more caring and nurturing an act than she would have given him credit for if the evidence wasn't right there for her to feel.

Shaking off the remains of sleep, she stretched. She was stiff and a little bit sore in places that hadn't been sore in a long while. And she detected a whiff of something from downstairs.

What was that? Steak, maybe.

He was cooking?

Huh. She was having trouble wrapping her head around that domesticated image of Rick.

Maybe if the cooking could be accomplished with tools worthy of a tough guy, such as a machete and flame thrower, then she might think he'd be up for it. But aprons and Cuisinarts? No. She couldn't picture Rick enjoying that.

Then again, he was ruled by his bodily urges and as he'd said, food was right up there with sex in the list of his top needs. Even cavemen had to eat. And to eat, at least anything hot, she supposed he'd have to cook because she sure as hell wasn't going to do it.

She shouldn't have to. She'd more than fulfilled his other need. She'd already done her part.

Though she supposed it was time to get up and shower, because two rounds with Rick had left her a sticky, sweaty mess. Then she could go downstairs and see what the hell was wafting up the staircase and making her stomach grumble with hunger.

Finally rallying the incentive, she pushed the itchy blanket down and swung her legs over the side of the mattress. She could only hope the sheets this cheap rental came with were nicer than that blanket. She didn't know since she and Rick had never actually made it under the covers, just on top of the bedspread.

Padding across the smooth hardwood floor barefooted, she bumped into something on the floor in the darkness. Feeling with her hands she realized he'd brought up her two bags.

In spite of everything, he could be a gentleman.

Good to know.

Sierra made her way to the hallway to find the bathroom, naked because she didn't care if he saw her. They'd moved far past that.

She found the bathroom thanks to the nightlight burning inside that cast a golden glow into the hall. She flipped on the switch for the overhead vanity lights.

On the counter next to the sink was a black case that had to be his.

Rick had been invading her privacy since she'd met him. Two could play at that game.

With a glance over her shoulder, she slowly, silently unzipped his case.

Inside she found a whole lot of nothing exciting. One glance told her he was a clean freak. Mouthwash. Dental floss. Toothbrush. Toothpaste. And if she wasn't mistaken, a tongue scraper. Okay, so the man took oral hygiene seriously.

Not a bad thing, considering she'd spent a good amount of time at the receiving end of his mouth today.

Further digging yielded a razor and some deodorant, vitamins, aspirin and not a whole hell of a lot more.

Sighing, she zipped the bag back up and moved toward the shower stall. She braced herself for the worst as she used one fingertip to push the shower curtain to the side.

But Rick had been right. The shower stall was perfectly clean. In fact, unlike the rest of the house, it looked as if it had actually been updated during this century.

Okay, she could deal with this. She'd just consider it like camping. A person had to deal with inconveniences in exchange for the pleasures.

In this case there was the water view right outside their back door . . . and, if Rick was to be believed, there was no stalker on their heels.

The perks pretty much ended there because she'd far rather be in a five-star hotel than a surf shack, but whatever. She was at the mercy of Rick, the Sun Tzu-reading, gun-toting chef. Not to mention sex machine.

Holy hell, he didn't even need recovery time. She'd have to take another look at that bottle of vitamins in his bag and see what was in them because they sure as hell worked for his stamina.

He was still a dickhead but hey, at least he knew where all the necessary parts were and what to do with them. If she'd have to put up with his attitude and his attempts to order her around and be in control of absolutely everything, including her and her cell phone, at least she'd be sexually satisfied while doing it.

She flipped on the hot water and went back to the bedroom. Opening her suitcase on the floor she grabbed her toiletry bag and some clothes.

Back in the bathroom, she stepped beneath the spray and was pleasantly surprised by some pretty kick ass water pressure. And it was hot enough to scald her, just the way she liked her showers. Hot.

One more point for the plus category in her Home, Sweet Shack.

He could have done worse in his choice for their accommodations. Of course, he also could have done better.

Starving now, thanks to Rick's culinary endeavors downstairs, she took one of the fastest showers of her life, not even taking the time to wash her hair before she flipped off the water.

She toweled off and pulled on the loose-fitting comfy clothes she'd unpacked.

Still smelling steak cooking, she padded down the staircase barefooted and turned the corner into the kitchen. There she saw Rick standing at the island stirring something in a big bowl with a wooden spoon. The counter was littered with his meal preparations. Onions. Mayonnaise. Mustard. She was a little speechless as she took in the scene.

Speechless but obviously not silent, since Rick glanced up almost the moment she reached the doorway."

"Hey, you're awake." He grinned wide, looking happy. To see her? To be cooking? She wasn't sure.

"Yes." She pushed off the doorway she'd been leaning against and moved toward him, eyeing the contents of the counter. She perched on one of the barstools lined up beneath the island counter. "I thought you wanted a sandwich."

"I ate that about three hours ago. It's time for dinner." His grin was so broad his eyes crinkled in the corners with it.

"You're in a good mood."

To prove her point, he let out a deep chuckle. "What's not to be in a good mood about? I've got all of my favorite things. Sex. Steak . . ."

She could tell he was baiting her. Almost daring her to comment on his crude sex talk. She decided for once, she wouldn't rise to the challenge he threw down.

"Wouldn't one less S-word in your lineup for today be nice?" she asked. When he frowned, obviously not getting what she was alluding to, she spelled it out for him. "Stalker."

He let out a snort of a laugh. "Stalker. Sniper. Yup, those are two S-words I could do without so I can enjoy the other two without worry."

The grin returned and she realized there was no bringing him down. He was giddy on sex and steak. She'd just have to take advantage of it.

"You brought my bags up to the bedroom for me."

"You pissed about that?" He raised his gaze from where he'd been chopping onions, looking almost hopeful that she might be.

Determined to not make this man happy, she shook her head. "No."

He picked up the onions and tossed them into a frying pan on the stovetop. They sizzled, dancing in the pan and sending a burst of steam into the air.

His comfort level in the kitchen was oddly fascinating. So much so she had to ask, "What exactly are you making?"

"Flank steak with sautéed onions and potato salad."

"Did you go out? I didn't notice potato salad when you unpacked the cooler."

He sent her a self-satisfied glance. "That's because I made it."

"You made it? From scratch?"

"Yes. It's not exactly rocket science. I boiled the

potatoes. We had the mayo and mustard for sandwiches. I threw in some chopped onions. Oh, and a splash of the salad dressing. For flavor." He reached into a drawer and pulled out a fork. Lifting a scoop from the bowl, he said, "Wanna try?"

"No, I'm good."

Rick didn't take no for an answer. He walked around the island, balancing the potato salad on the fork while he held one hand beneath it. "Come on. Try it."

He brought the fork to her lips, leaving her no choice but to open her mouth and take the food in.

Her eyes widened at the flavors on her tongue when she'd been expecting the usual bland potato salad. "Wow. That's good."

His smile reached all the way to his eyes again. It seemed this man didn't do anything half way. Not cooking. Not smiling. Not in bed.

She swallowed as her mouth started to water in anticipation of the steak and onions, whose aroma filled the kitchen.

He moved back around the island and, lifting the pan, flipped the contents with one flick of a wrist. It was like having front row seats to a cooking show. Except she knew how the chef's tongue tasted . . . and felt.

Sierra cleared her throat, hoping to clear that memory from her brain before she did something foolish, like asking him if he'd sleep in her bed tonight.

Sleep. That was an amusing thought. She doubted there'd be a whole lot of that if he spent the night in her bed.

"Almost ready. Just letting the steak rest for a few minutes before I cut it and waiting for the onions to caramelize."

Caramelized onions? "What in the world do you know about caramelized onions? Who *are* you?"

Rick let out a snort. "I'm a man who likes to eat, who has a roommate who doesn't like to cook, so I didn't have all that much choice in the matter. It was learn my way around the kitchen or live on take-out food. Now that I'm not working out as much as I used to it's easy to pack on the pounds eating too much take-out."

She eyed the width of his shoulders. The way his muscles flexed and relaxed as he went through the motions of preparing the meal. This was what Rick looked like when he wasn't working out as hard as he used to? What the hell did he used to look like?

"So do you want to talk about your case now or after we eat?" Rick asked.

His question surprised her. She hadn't realized there was anything about her case to discuss. As far as she knew, they were stuck here until the police or Rick's boss or someone of some authority told her it was safe to go back.

Or until the movie studio threatened to sue her for breech of contract and she was legally forced to return to set, which was a very real possibility.

This little poorly timed sabbatical just before they were about to wrap the movie was not going to work in her favor when it came to negotiating her pay for the next one. It wouldn't matter that it hadn't been her fault, or even her choice.

It was in the best interest of her career to get

back to work as soon as possible. That was inspiration enough to have this conversation with Rick about any progress in the case right away.

"Let's discuss it now."

He tipped his head. "All right. While you were sleeping I talked to Jon—"

On the phone he was allowed to have when she wasn't. That had her gritting her teeth a bit as she asked, "And?"

"They're making progress."

"Progress how?" What could they possibly have to go on? A broken doorframe on her trailer from a bullet shot by an unseen shooter? A bullet that only Rick felt.

"They've got a crew pawing through your fan mail from the past year."

"What crew? Who? The police?"

"Actually, it's Jon, Zane, Jon's girlfriend Ali, and Darci." He cringed as his gaze pinned hers. "You okay with that? I know it's an invasion of your privacy, but Roger approved it. They really did need full access to your fan mail to figure this thing out."

That was what he was worried about? His boss, friends and family reading her fan mail? Meanwhile he knew all about her current choice in birth control thanks to him and his brutish buddies traipsing through her bathroom before dawn.

"It's fine. *I* don't even read my fan mail. We hire an assistant to open it and answer it for me. As me, actually, so the fans won't know the response isn't from me personally."

He put down the spoon he'd been stirring the onions with. "Really? That's interesting."

"Why is that interesting?" Her defenses went up immediately. "Go on. Make some comment about how fake I am or how dishonest that is to the fans who support me."

His brows rose high. "Whoa. Dial it back, princess. It's interesting because whoever answered that mail as you might have inadvertently encouraged this guy in their reply. What you didn't let me tell you yet is that Jon flagged a bunch of letters. He's very interested in one batch in particular. Since it wasn't you who responded, maybe we need to track down and talk to whoever answered those letters to see if they encouraged him in some way."

One word caught her attention. "Letters. Plural?"

"Yeah." He drew in a breath, as if he knew she wasn't going to like the answer. "Three dozen."

"Three dozen?" Her voice rose high. "Over how long of a period?"

"Six months."

Holy moly. As she panicked, Rick already had his phone out.

He punched in a text then set the phone on the island before raising his gaze to her. "You okay?"

"I'm not sure." If she had a definitive yes or no, she would have said so but right now, that was the most honest answer she could come up with. "Who did you just text?"

"Jon. To tell him to get on finding who replied to your fan mail during that period." Rick moved around the island.

He wrapped his arms around her and she let him pull her tight against a chest too hard to be comfortable, yet it made her feel better anyway.

That she let him hold her—and she liked it—was testament of how freaked out she was about those dozens of letters she hadn't known existed until now.

Pressed against his chest she breathed in the scent of him. Clean man and some masculine scented deodorant mingled with the smells of the cooking food that clung to his shirt.

"Sierra, listen to me. This is good. It's a solid lead. We'll wrap this case up and have you back to work in no time."

She managed to nod.

Rick rubbed his hand up and down her back, soothing her. Nothing sexual. Just nice. He pulled back enough to look down at her. "I'm gonna cut the steak and make you a plate."

"I don't know if I can eat."

Her stomach was twisting, making her feel ill from the thought of this person writing to her so incessantly. And not one of her staff thought that was a red flag? She needed to seriously evaluate her personnel.

She glanced up to find Rick watching her closely.

"Stop." He said it in a firm deep tone that left no doubt he wanted her to obey.

Too bad for him, she had no clue what it was he wanted her to stop doing. She was just sitting there.

"Stop what?"

"Obsessing. Worrying. Thinking. The police and my guys are all on this. There's nothing you can do except take care of yourself. You're going to eat—

your body needs the food—then you're going to take one of those sleeping pills of yours and you're going to get a good night's sleep because that nap didn't make up for the sleep you lost last night. And no I didn't paw through your bag. I saw the bottle in the bathroom at the hotel."

He certainly was observant about details, right down to what medications her doctor prescribed. For some reason, she didn't hate that as much as she should.

Maybe in the absence of all else, a person had to take what they could get. Rick was the only friend—and the only protection—she had right now. The one man standing between her and whoever was stalking her.

Or maybe it was just that the shoulder holster and accompanying gun he was once again wearing had become oddly comforting to her.

Like it or not, he was also the only man in her life available to hold her and make her forget everything, if even for a little while. She knew he'd dedicate all two hundred plus pounds of himself doing that, if she just asked.

"You agree to all that?" he asked.

Rick was focused on her, concern clear in his expression, while she was torn between being frightened to death and obsessed with having more sex with him.

"Okay. I'll try to eat and later I'll take a sleeping pill. But there's something I wouldn't mind doing in between. If you're up for it." She raised her gaze to meet his hoping he'd get the hint. That he wouldn't make her outright ask.

The corner of his mouth tipped up. "Yeah. That sounds good."

He dropped his hold on her and made his way around the island, but not without a backward glance that had his smile broadening.

She was pretty sure he understood exactly what she needed.

CHAPTER EIGHTEEN

Sierra came into the bedroom carrying a prescription pill bottle in one hand. Rick slid off the shoulder holster and laid it on the dresser as he watched her put the bottle on the table next to the cold water he had carried upstairs for her.

He looked from the table to her, his hand poised on the button at the waist of his pants. "I hope you didn't take one of those sleeping pills quite yet."

"No. Don't worry." She glanced over her shoulder at him, her tone indulgent.

"Oh, I wasn't really worried." Pill or not, he figured he would have been able to keep her attention for as long as he needed it.

He'd let her get a good night's sleep eventually, but right now he was going to distract her and himself for a little while.

Or maybe a long while.

She'd eaten. Not everything on her plate but enough to make him happy she had something decent in her stomach. But she was worried, he could tell, and he had every plan to help her forget this stalker.

She dropped her clothes and he had the pleasure of gazing upon her. From the tips of her painted toes, all the way up to the peaks of her pink-tipped breasts. Not to mention all of the smooth silky bare skin in between.

Hell, he'd just about forgotten her stalker too, just from seeing her like this. "Were you naked under those clothes all through dinner?"

"Yes. Why?" She glanced back at him as she flipped back the covers on the bed.

"I'm just glad I didn't know that then." Knowing she wasn't wearing any underwear or bra would have been too tempting. He would have had to set her up on the island and do nasty but oh so nice things to her.

That would have been a very bad idea. Not because he didn't enjoy mixing things up in different locations besides the bedroom once in a while, but there were too many damn windows downstairs.

She crawled onto the mattress and flipped over, sending him a heated glance. "What would you have done if you'd known?"

"I'll show you." Inspired, Rick sped up his own disrobing.

There were far too many clothes between them, and at the moment, they were all his.

As he pulled his shirt off he moved toward the bed. He shed and dropped the remainder of his clothes as he went so he was naked by the time he reached her.

They'd gotten along well all through dinner. No bitching or smart ass comments from her. No provoking her from his end. He'd kind of enjoyed the angry sex, but he was willing to give this a try too.

Chances were this new peace between them would only be a temporary truce anyway. Either way he'd have Sierra sighing beneath him.

Rick kneeled on the mattress and moved until he sat straddling her legs.

She moved, forcing him to move with her until he had his back against the headboard and she straddled him. Leaning forward she cupped his face in her hands and pressed a kiss to his mouth.

He hadn't thought it possible but this hard-as-nails woman could be soft and gentle when she wanted to be.

The kiss was sweet but thorough . . . and then she bit him.

"Ow." He pulled back and ran his tongue over his lip, tasting for blood.

Sierra smirked. "Don't tell me that hurt a big tough guy like you."

She ran the tip of one finger over the bruise she'd left when she'd bit him earlier. That bite had been much harder, but since he'd been occupied at the time it hadn't bothered him at all. Hell, he'd nearly shot off from the feel of her teeth sinking into him.

Her stare swept down his body followed by her hand, from the mark on his chest to his abs.

He decided to let the damage she'd done to his lip go without further comment as she ran her fingers over the dusting of hair on his stomach. His breath caught in his throat as she moved her hand lower and grasped him. Then she lowered her head.

Damn.

He hissed in a breath as she scraped her teeth up his length, but there was no way he was going to stop her. He'd spent too much time picturing those lips wrapped around him while she'd been flapping them at him with one complaint or another to complain now.

Besides, two could play at this game. Soon he'd have her on her back and he'd be inflicting some torture of his own.

She had him nearing the zone to finish this when his phone buzzed.

"Fuck." He'd laid the burner cell, his only connection to GAPS, on the nightstand. It was close enough to reach, but the last thing he wanted to do was be interrupted now as the heat of Sierra's mouth engulfed him.

Ignoring a communication during a mission was so wrong it could have gotten him in deep shit when he'd been in the teams. Rick knew that, but he let the phone buzz on. He'd call back.

Without missing a stroke, Sierra reached out and grabbed the phone. Apparently, she was not as intent on ignoring the call as he was. She slid off his cock long enough to hit to answer the call and then tossed the phone onto his chest and went right back to what she'd been doing.

Shit. Now he had to talk. Trying to not sound as if he was doing what he was doing, Rick blew out a breath and then pressed the cell to his ear. "Yeah."

"Hey." Jon's voice came through the earpiece.

Rick loved this man like a brother but the last thing he wanted to be doing right now is talking to him. "Hey."

"You okay? Is everything good there?"

"Yeah, it's all good here. Sorry. I was uh, just working out. I'm a little out of breath." Rick felt Sierra's chuckle vibrate straight through his cock. He needed to wrap up this call. "What's up?"

"I got news."

"Yeah?" Rick pulled the phone away from his face as she chose that moment to add both hands to the mix of what she was already doing to him with her mouth.

The combination of sensations was enough to have him squeezing his eyes closed as he clenched his teeth to stop from making a sound. That would be sure to tip off Jon that it wasn't exercise that had him breathless.

"We turned those letters over to the cops. There's no return address but all of them required additional postage because he was sending her homemade cards and pressed flowers and shit, so he actually had to go to the post office and have them weighed. They think because of that they've got enough to find an address on the guy. As soon as they do, they're moving in. We might have you home again tomorrow."

"Wow. Okay. Keep me informed."

"You got it. I'll call in the morning."

"Yeah. Bye." Rick cut off the call with the bare minimum of formalities and tossed the cell onto the mattress.

Holy shit, this woman had some crazy skills.

His willpower was no match for her or her probing fingers and apparent lack of a gag reflex. She seemed to double her efforts the moment he hung up with Jon.

There was no more need for Rick to remain quiet.

A shout he couldn't have controlled even if he wanted to burst from him as Sierra never let up, riding out his orgasm like a champion.

Finally, she flopped onto her back next to him. "Who was on the phone?"

He laughed. He was barely able to breathe yet and she wanted to talk. "Jon."

"What's happening with the case?"

"He's going to call with an update in the morning." Rick swiveled his head toward her, trying not to feel guilty.

It wasn't exactly a lie. Just a selection of the truth. That wasn't so bad.

What was bad, however, was his secret hope that the police would take their time locating this guy, because the last thing he wanted to do was leave their humble love shack anytime soon.

The countdown clock to the end was now ticking.

With that in mind, Rick rolled over on top of Sierra. He scraped his teeth over the delicate flesh of one rosy nipple treating her to the same exquisite torture she'd employed on him. And just like him, she liked it—he felt the tremor run through her.

They were a good match, him and her, in the verbal sparring arena and in bed.

He moved down her body, again silently willing the police to take their time and give him at least a couple more days. But then, a month of this might not be enough time for him to have had his fill of Sierra.

Rick absorbed every nuance of her as he worked his way over her body with hands and mouth. The silky smooth warmth of her skin. The scent of her, part clean soap and part aroused woman. The sound of her gasp as he spread her legs and bowed his head to taste of her. The tremble in her thighs and eventually the sound of her cries as he pushed her over the edge.

But he wasn't ready to ease off of her yet.

He pushed her further until she squirmed to get away from him, eventually giving in to his will as she let him drive her higher.

Finally, she writhed away from him.

Gasping she pushed at his head. "Too much."

It was never too much, in his opinion, but he let her off easy and pulled himself up the bed, flopping onto his back next to her.

That's when the damn phone buzzed again somewhere amid the rumpled and tangled sheets.

She wiggled, reached beneath her and emerged with his cell phone. He stuck his hand out for her to hand it over, but she didn't. Instead, she squinted at the display.

"It's from Jon. *Tango located. Moving in.*" Sierra

spun her head to face him. "What's that mean?"

Rick let out a sigh of resignation. The honeymoon was over. Or at least would be very soon. "It means the police found the guy sending you all those letters and they're going to get him."

Her eyes widened. "So it's over? We can go home?"

"Not quite yet, but yeah, probably soon."

"Like tomorrow?"

"Maybe."

"Thank God. Roger and the studio will be very happy to hear that."

Unfortunately, Rick was not equally as excited by Jon's good news. He watched her roll toward the nightstand and reach for the pill bottle but before she could reach, he grabbed her by the hips and pulled her until her back pressed against his chest.

"Don't take that yet." He was counting their remaining time together in hours now instead of days and he wasn't going to waste any of it.

Rick was more than ready. His cock only knew she was close, not how close he was to saying goodbye to her sweet body.

He didn't wait for permission as he plunged into her wet heat.

CHAPTER NINETEEN

Sierra woke to the sound of the shower running. She hadn't felt Rick get out of bed. She was usually a light sleeper, but last night at Rick's urging she'd taken a sleeping pill.

Of course, he'd only let her take the pill after he'd already worn her out the old fashioned way.

She stretched and felt even more sore than she had last night.

Muscles she hadn't worked in a long time protested, aching as she moved to get herself up and out of the bed.

She'd slept but the residual effect of the sleeping pill left her feeling groggy.

Typical sedative hangover. She needed coffee.

Uh, oh? Had Rick brought coffee?

Her brain was running a bit slow so she had to

think. She'd only really seen him unloading the cooler, and she'd seen what he'd had out to cook dinner last night. She didn't know everything else he might have brought.

God, she hoped there was a nice fresh pound of grinds down there. She didn't even care what brand. She'd drink it and be happy.

If he hadn't he'd just have to go out and get coffee, or else she'd go herself and she wouldn't care who recognized her.

A memory hit her as her brain slowly woke. She recalled a text from Jon to Rick about moving in on the stalker.

Today could end her captivity.

That realization was almost as good as caffeine to wake her up and get her moving.

Smiling just at the thought of going back to work and feeling safe again, she grabbed the closest thing she could find. Rick's T-shirt. She pulled it over her nakedness and didn't bother with anything else.

She'd have to come up and shower as soon as he was done, so why get dressed? He'd rented the whole shack so they'd have privacy and she intended to take advantage of it.

Feeling lighter than she had in days, Sierra padded down the stairs in bare feet, turned the corner and got smacked with one hell of a view.

Inside the kitchen she paused in her pursuit of caffeine to take in the intense color of the sky and the water as the sun rose over the horizon. She knew the water was out there, but it wasn't until now she'd taken the time to appreciate it.

She enjoyed the vista as she tried to think like

Rick and figure out where he might have stashed the coffee.

If she were a food obsessed brute with an unhealthy controlling streak and surprising kitchen skills, where would she stash the coffee?

She glanced around the kitchen and added *neat freak* to her list of descriptions for Rick. Everything was clean and organized, put away in its proper place as if he hadn't cooked a big meal just twelve hours before.

Her gaze hit on a coffeemaker plugged into the wall on the counter beneath a row of overhead cabinets. Holding her breath, Sierra hoped for the best and pulled open the door just above the coffeemaker.

She smiled wide. There it was, a bag of coffee grinds, just as she suspected it might be. Where else would Mr. Organized put the coffee but above the maker?

Okay, so he was both annoying and handy to have around. She had grown enough over the past few days to be able to admit that freely about her bodyguard.

There was a package of filters next to the bag of coffee. She didn't know if Rick had brought them or if they came with the rental, but she was grateful the filters were there.

Luckily, the coffeemaker was one of the idiot-proof kinds. Water there. Filter and grinds there. One button to push. Done.

Nothing to do but wait and that wasn't even for very long. The simple but hardworking maker chugged along and shortly announced its job complete with a pop and a hiss.

Opening the door of the fridge, Sierra found Rick had brought a small container of whole milk. Good enough. Beggars couldn't be choosers. She'd save her soymilk lattes for when she was at Starbucks. Here, seaside in a surf shack rental, good old-fashioned whole milk seemed to fit.

Another pull of a door and Sierra found the glassware and dishes. She grabbed a mug and poured herself a steaming hot cup, then splashed some milk into the cup's black depths.

After searching a couple of drawers, she found a spoon, gave the mug a stir and was done. He hadn't brought artificial sweetener but that would have been too much to ask. She could do without.

She brought the mug to her lips, drew in the aroma of the brew and finally she was ready to take her first blessed sip.

Now that coffee had been acquired, she wanted to see the view without the salt spray coating the windows obscuring it.

It took having to put the mug down and her using two hands against the stuck door to loosen the swollen wood but after a second it released, sending her stumbling. She reached for her mug on the table by the door and headed out into the sunshine.

Facing the water, she closed her eyes, tilted her head back and absorbed the incredible feel of the warmth of the sun on her face while breathing in the fresh air.

There was water in Miami, where she called home when she wasn't on the road nine months out of the year, but Miami was a city.

This . . . this was almost deserted. There were houses, yes, but at this time of morning and in early March, it felt like she was the only person on the island.

Sierra moved forward, cradling the mug between her hands to absorb the warmth. The heat of the day had yet to take hold and there was a nip in the air. The little bit of a breeze off the water wrapped the bottom of Rick's shirt tight to her thighs.

Taking another sip she stared out at the water and listened to the sound of the birds. It was a near perfect morning.

When was the last time she'd had one of those?

Hard to enjoy nature when she was in a hotel behind black out curtains. Or to enjoy the morning when she was rushing to get to the studio and into the makeup chair.

Maybe after this movie was done she should take a trip, if she could wedge it in before the start of the next movie, which would be followed by the press tour for this one.

Fame. Money. She had everything she always thought she'd wanted. Funny that once she had it all, it turned out what she really wanted was just a little bit of peace.

"Good morning." Rick's deep voice directly behind her had Sierra glancing over her shoulder to frown at him.

"Stop sneaking up on me."

He snorted. "I didn't sneak. I walked. Pretty damn loudly too, if you ask me. You were just too busy sighing at the water to hear me."

She looked back to the view now, preferring that

to arguing with him over something pointless.

He took a step forward and she could see he was not only fully dressed, but already in full guard dog mode. He scanned the dunes on either side of them from behind his dark sunglasses.

When he determined they weren't in imminent danger from an attack from either flank, he glanced down at her. She watched his brows draw low.

"Is that my shirt?"

"Yes. Why? You mad I'm wearing it?"

One corner of his mouth quirked up. "No, princess. Not one bit."

She could feel his stare on her even through his dark glasses.

"Are you wearing anything under it?" he asked.

"No." She waited for the reprimand. The order to get inside and put on clothes, or something equally bossy.

It didn't come. What did was a curse muttered beneath his breath followed by him shaking his head. She was about to ask him what was the matter, when he reached down and adjusted himself through the fabric of his pants, which told her exactly what was bothering him.

Who was in control now? That would be *her*. She smiled and took another sip of coffee.

"Any word from Jon?" she asked.

She wouldn't hate staying another day, especially now that she'd tamed her guard dog, but she really did need to get back to the set.

"Nope. It's still early."

She turned away from the view with a sigh. "I suppose I should shower and get my stuff together so when the call does come we can leave for Virginia right away."

"You're anxious to leave." He turned with her and followed as she led the way to the house.

"Uh, huh. That way I can get my life back, and get rid of you. I'm taking a shower." Glancing back, she saw a strange expression cross his face. "Don't worry. I'll leave your shirt where I found it."

"Fine." His tone was flat as he said it.

She wasn't awake enough to analyze Rick's moods. All she cared about was that phone call telling her it was safe to come back. This little sex-filled retreat from reality had been fun, but she was very anxious to shake the hired shadow trailing behind her twenty-four seven. That part of this whole situation she wouldn't miss.

Taking her mug with her, she made her way back towards the stairs. She might come back to the island again. But next time, she was renting something far less shack-like.

"Hello?" The sound of Rick answering his phone had Sierra spinning back toward the kitchen so fast the coffee sloshed out of the mug and onto her hand.

She shook the liquid off as she strode toward the kitchen. "What?"

Frowning he silently shushed her, which only made her want to know more who was on the phone and what they were saying.

"You feel good about this?" He paused after the question, while Sierra moved closer, dying to know who felt good about what.

Maybe if she got close enough, she'd be able to

hear—

Not having it, Rick turned away and walked toward the back door.

How rude.

Scowling, she watched, but didn't pursue him. Obnoxious control freak that he was, he'd probably rather go out and talk in the surf than let her hear.

He listened to the person on the other end of the line for what felt like forever before he finally said, "All right. See you in a few."

Turning back, he shoved the phone in his pocket and met her gaze. "You get your wish, princess."

"We're going back?" The excitement of that news had her voice rising high.

"Yup." He strode across the kitchen and sidled around her to move through the doorway. He turned toward the staircase and, taking the stairs two at a time, disappeared upstairs.

CHAPTER TWENTY

Get back into work mode.

Be professional.

Become detached—the way he should have remained the whole damn time.

That's what Rick had to do because only an idiot got involved with the client while working a close-protection security detail.

He was, by all proof, an idiot. Especially for thinking that what they'd shared had affected Sierra in any way.

Pfft. She was more anxious to get away from him, or more accurately to have him get away from her, than ever.

Sierra reached out and spun the knob of the radio on the dashboard, quieting the rock music blaring out of the speakers. "You're awfully quiet."

The princess speaks . . .

After she'd played with her cell phone for literally hours when Rick finally allowed her to turn it on, he'd doubted she was going to say a word the whole trip.

Of course, he hadn't helped things by turning the radio up too loud for normal conversation. But just because they hadn't been talking didn't mean he could forget she was there. She seemed to permeate his senses.

What was that scent? Shampoo? He'd used her shampoo in the shower and he didn't smell like that. Perfume maybe? Whatever it was had memories creeping through the wall he'd tried to erect in his brain. He was defenseless.

He hated that.

It had been a long three and a half hours together in the car. Good thing the bulk of the trip was behind them.

"Just paying attention to the road."

The road taking him home to his dead end job and the house he lived in with his sister.

"You know, you never answered me."

He glanced sideways at her confusing accusation. "Never answered you about what?"

"Your family."

"You still want to know more about my family?" The only reason Rick could think of why she'd be talking to him at all, and about his family, was that she must be incredibly bored.

"Yes, I told you I did. Why do you have such trouble believing that?"

This coming from the woman who could be

tangled up with him for twelve out of twenty-four hours and then walk away without a backward glance.

He kept his opinion on her self centered nature to himself.

"Fine. You want to know, I'll tell you. It's a riveting story so you might want to brace yourself." He glanced over in time to see her wrinkle her nose at him.

Damn, she looked cute sometimes. Cute enough he almost forgot about her cold heart.

Rick cleared his throat. "Well, Mom and Dad are empty nesters now so they're enjoying life. Hiking the Grand Canyon. They took a cruise through the Panama Canal on New Years Eve. They're acting like they're a couple of newlyweds."

It was honestly a little bit sickening. Especially the time he found them making out in the kitchen last time he visited. He could have lived a whole life without seeing that.

"And your sister?"

He shrugged. "We get on each others nerves but I love her anyway."

Not so much the other night when Darci and Chris had been at it, once again, at two a.m. and Rick had to be to work at six. If he had to hear her and Chris banging the headboard against the wall one more time, he might have to toss her bed off the back deck.

Out of the corner of his eye, he saw Sierra pursing her lips.

"What?" he asked.

"Exactly as I expected. Your family is perfect."

Was she serious? "Perfect? Yeah, right."

"Yup. You said you'd trust your sister with your life."

"Yeah. So? You can always trust family." In spite of how they sometimes bickered like they hated each other.

She snorted. "First of all, I know for a fact you can't always trust family so that whole statement just went right out the window. And I can tell you, your family is abnormal, because most families I've seen are pretty messed up."

"Okay." Raising a brow at her vehemence, he decided it would be best to just agree with her.

Something had definitely happened. Since she'd been famous since she was barely a teenager, he figured there was a good chance whatever had happened would be public. Rick made a mental note to dig a little deeper into Sierra's history online.

The scenery speeding past the car windows began to look familiar as they neared Hampton Roads. They'd be saying goodbye in no time, then Sierra wouldn't have to worry about him or his supposedly abnormally perfect family.

"Roger has you booked at a new hotel. Jon was going to text him this morning so he knew about when to expect us today. He should be waiting for you."

"How much longer until we get there?" she asked, glancing over.

"Fifteen minutes, depending on traffic." Then Rick could dump the princess and her suitcase off and get back to his regularly scheduled programming.

"Okay. Great." She whipped out her ever present cell phone and focused on the screen. Probably to Tweet or Facebook or whatever the hell she posted on that made every damn minute and event of her life public fodder.

Though not every moment. She wouldn't put what had happened between him and her on there.

That wouldn't be fit for public consumption. He wasn't some star or billionaire. He was just her security. Their time together would no doubt remain her dirty little secret. Just like it all never happened.

The final miles passed in silence. Rick stewing in his own bad mood. Sierra doing whatever she did that made her Sierra Cox, social media darling.

It wasn't long before he spotted the hotel and pulled off the highway and into the drive.

He eyed the location critically. A tall building bracketed by the water and the highway with not much of anything else around save for the convention center. He supposed it was better than the last hotel with the tall building directly across from Sierra's suite that anyone could use as a vantage point.

And it didn't really matter anymore what he thought, did it? This case was over just like his association with her would be the moment he turned her over to her manager and drove away.

Rick pulled beneath the overhead canopy in front of the hotel. "We're here."

She glanced up and looked at the front entrance. It probably wasn't up to snuff, in her opinion, but she didn't say anything. She just reached for the door handle.

"Whoa. Hang on there, princess."

She turned to frown at him. "What now?"

What now? Yeah, because he'd demanded so much of her today . . . "Wait until I text Roger and tell him to get down here."

The furrow in her brow deepened. "I can get to my room myself. And look. There's a bellhop right there. He'll take my bag."

Rick wasn't worried about the damn bag, which was on wheels anyway. "Please. Humor me one last time. Then I'll be out of your life forever. Promise."

Yeah, those words didn't taste bitter at all.

Drawing in a deep breath, she flopped back against the seat. "Fine. Text him."

He did, and good old Roger texted right back. "He's on his way down."

"Good. Can I get out of the car and stretch my legs, at least? Or must I stay in my seat securely fastened?"

Rick rolled his eyes at her dramatic exaggeration. "You can get out." He had to get out anyway so he could pop the trunk and get her stuff out.

"Sierra!" Roger strode across the short distance between the glass entrance doors and the car. "It's so good to have you back."

He pulled her into his arms and hugged her so tightly she laughed. "Roger, I can't breathe."

Rick was having a similar reaction to watching the hug. It seemed to hurt to breathe as he thought how he'd been doing more than just holding her about this time yesterday.

"Sorry. I'm just happy you're safe." Roger

pulled away, but maintained his hold on her shoulders as he looked her up and down, as if to assure himself she really was okay.

"I'm fine. He had me cloistered away on an island where the only way on or off was by boat or plane."

"Really?" Roger lifted his brows and moved his focus from Sierra to Rick. "Sounds like heaven."

Sierra let out a snort filled with derision. "If heaven is a surfside shack that hasn't been redecorated since the seventies, then yeah. It was heaven."

"Retro is in, sweetie. Keep up with the times." Roger dropped his hold on Sierra and moved toward where Rick stood by the open trunk. He extended his hand. "Thanks for taking care of her."

And there came the guilt, because Rick had done far more with Sierra than protect her. What they'd done together gave *close-security* a whole new meaning.

Rick accepted the man's hand, but not his thanks. "Just doing my job."

His job as her bodyguard. Oh, he'd guarded Sierra's body, all right.

"Well, I appreciate it anyway. And I'll make sure to tell your boss that."

Rick controlled the smile and nodded. "Thanks."

He and *his boss* had been to hell and back, a few times, over their years in the teams. After surviving BUD/S together, and DEVGRU, somehow Rick didn't think Jon would be performing annual employment evaluations on him.

Apparently done with the hired help, Roger

turned back to Sierra. "Ready to get back to work tomorrow?"

"You don't even know how ready. Are the producers mad at me? And the director must be livid I threw off the schedule." She cringed.

"Not at all. They'd rather have you miss two days of shooting than be—you know—actually shot."

She laughed. "I guess so. Good point."

As he slipped her carry-on over his shoulder and grabbed the handle on the suitcase, Rick held back the comment that the shooting was nothing to laugh about. It was a real fucking threat and she and her manager should be taking it more seriously.

"Here you go." Rick set the suitcase on the ground by Sierra and handed the shoulder bag to Roger. "You all set here?"

"I think we're good." Roger answered his question then directed his attention to Sierra. "I got you the best suite they had. Nice view of the water out the back."

Good. A view of the water meant no building to act as a sniper hide with a bead on Sierra's window.

Rick didn't mention that. This case was closed.

The police had arrested the fan who'd sent Sierra all those letters. And they'd recovered proof from his residence—photos of her.

The case should be over.

So why was Rick's sixth sense stabbing at his brain like a red hot poker?

He drew in a breath and pushed the sensation aside. He had to get through this goodbye first. He could obsess over the source of his worry after that.

"I'm, uh, gonna take off."

Roger turned to Rick one more time. "Thanks again."

"You're welcome." Again. Rick looked at Sierra. "So, good luck with the uh, you know, movie and all."

"Thanks." She stepped forward and surprised him with a tight warm hug that pressed her soft body against his from tits to thighs.

Christ, that felt good. He didn't want to let her go. But after a squeeze in return, he stepped back. "Bye."

"Bye." She turned immediately back to Roger. "Do you think I should meet with the director today? Just to see if we can juggle the schedule a bit to make up for the missed days."

Rick strode around the car. She'd already gotten back to her life. Time to get back to his.

Through his sunglasses from behind the wheel of the car he watched her walk away. He remained there until he could no longer see her through the glass doors of the lobby. Only then could he bring himself to start the engine and drive away.

Fuck.

CHAPTER TWENTY-ONE

"Hey, bro. Good to have you back." Chris jumped up from the sofa to greet Rick the moment he pushed through the front door. He grabbed Rick in a one armed, back slapping hug.

"Thanks." Rick dumped his duffle on the floor. He'd have to get the cooler out of the trunk, unload the leftover food from his little trip, and then put his weapons back in the safe. Or maybe not. "Hey, after I get the car unloaded, you want to go to the range?"

He had the sudden urge to shoot something. That might get rid of some of this excess energy. Settle his mind.

"Yeah, sure." Chris nodded, following Rick out the door to the car parked in the driveway. He grabbed one end of the cooler out of the trunk while Rick grabbed the other.

"You have to ask Darci first?" Rick tried to keep the judgment out of his voice as he'd asked it. Though the term *pussy whipped* did come to mind.

"Nah, she's at work."

Rick paused. "She's at work and you're here alone?"

Chris stopped too, mainly because Rick had the other end of the cooler. "Yeah. I was waiting on a load of laundry. Darci's sheets."

Rick couldn't help that his brows shot up at that info. Hanging out and watching TV when no one was home. Doing laundry—the sheets Chris had no doubt sweated up last night with Darci. Was Chris living here now and Rick just hadn't gotten the memo?

Chris drew in a breath. "Look, dude. If you have a problem with me being here so much—"

Rick shook his head, cutting off Chris. "No. I'm sorry. I really don't. I'm just stressed from the drive."

"I'm really here because I knew you were on your way home and I wanted to talk to you. The laundry was just an afterthought. I swear, dude."

"It's okay. Really. I wanna run over Sierra's case too. That is what you wanted to talk to me about, right?"

"Yeah. Things don't feel right."

"I know. That's exactly how I feel."

Chris nodded. "Come on. Get this shit inside, then we'll head to the range and I'll fill you in on everything in the truck."

That was the best plan Rick had heard all day. "Sounds good."

In the kitchen, they set the cooler on the floor. Rick opened the lid and the Pandora's box worth of memories it contained.

He would have left all the extra food in North Carolina if there hadn't been a note to renters on the fridge saying they had to remove everything before leaving.

As he took out the open carton of milk he'd carried home from the beach house Rick did his best to not remember Sierra's lips wrapped around that coffee mug this morning.

That image led directly into the memory of her lips wrapped around his cock. Yeah, that was not good on any level, but especially bad with Chris standing next to him.

Time to change the subject "So, you need to stop home and get your bag before we hit the range?"

"Nah, I have my range bag in the truck, and my guns on me."

Rick glanced up. Sure enough, Chris was wearing his waist holster and probably his leg holster too. That wasn't something he made a habit of doing, as far as Rick knew.

"Something up?" Rick asked.

"Maybe. Maybe not." Chris glanced in the cooler. "Let's finish this shit and get going."

"Okay." Curious now, Rick did exactly that.

A few more items stowed away and Rick had the cooler out on the back deck, dumped upside down and drying in the sun.

Chris stood, keys in his hand by the front door. "Ready?"

"More than ready." Rick scooped up his

weapons bag and followed Chris outside.

Inside the truck, Chris pulled onto the main road and then shot Rick a glance. "So, we turned those letters over to the cops."

Rick nodded. "Yup. That I heard."

"Well, they tracked down the guy easy enough. It seems he's at the same post office like once a week, bragging to the clerks how Sierra Cox is his girlfriend. He has a damn post office box there, so of course his home address was on file."

"Wow. That seems too fucking easy."

"Exactly what I thought. So they go to the guy's place and bring him in. Easy, no struggle, no fight in him. He's happy to go and talk to them. They also search the apartment and yeah, they find pictures, which the cops take as proof. But there's one problem."

When Chris paused and glanced across the cab, Rick asked, "What problem?"

"Not a one of those pictures was taken from that camera we found inside her bathroom. Not one even matched the pictures delivered to her trailer in that envelope. They're all far away, fuzzy shots taken while she was out in public. Coming out of some boutique carrying a shopping bag. Going into a coffee shop. Getting into her limo."

"Shots anyone could take without having access to her room."

Chris tipped his head. "Yup. Now, here is the kicker. Ask me where the guy they arrested lives."

"I'm going to assume not around here."

"Nope. In fucking Florida. Right where they arrested him."

"He have an alibi for two days ago when Sierra was targeted at the lot?"

"He's a loner who does odd jobs, so no. No alibi, which the police are using as proof they got the right guy. He owns a car so they say he could have driven here, taken that shot at Sierra, then driven back home."

Rick drew in a breath. "Why would he leave town? The job wasn't finished."

"That's what I'm thinking."

"How do you know all this?" Rick asked.

"I took the cop we were working here with out for drinks last night. We bonded. He's ex-Navy. So late this morning I get a call. It's him inviting me to come to the precinct to take a look-see at the photos of the evidence found in the suspect's apartment in Florida."

Rick shook his head as Chris swung the truck into a parking space in the shooting range lot. "You and your damn southern charm."

The man always could talk his way out of any situation and into any door he wanted.

Chris shot Rick a grin as he pulled the keys out of the ignition. "You complaining?"

"Hell, no." But Rick didn't like what Chris had found out.

The cops were shoving all of this evidence into a neat little box marked *guilty* when none of it proved anything except that the guy liked to take pictures of her in public and send Sierra letters. And maybe he was a little—or a lot—delusional about the closeness of their relationship.

What if the cops were wrong and the shooter was

still out there? It explained why Chris was walking around armed and why Rick couldn't shake the feeling something was wrong.

When they were both out of the truck and crossing the parking lot, heading for the door, Rick asked, "Did you tell Jon all this?"

Chris shook his head. "Jon and Zane are on a flight to HOA. They left this morning right after they got the call about the arrest. That was before I met with the cop."

Shit. Jon and Zane would be out of touch for hours. It might be two days worth of flights and layovers before they got to Djibouti. And even after they landed, they'd probably be too busy to be checking in on a case that everyone except Chris and Rick considered closed.

Still it wouldn't hurt to shoot them an email in the hopes one of them would check. Rick opened his mouth to say exactly that when Chris squinted past him. "Any reason there would be a car tailing us?"

"What?" Rick spun to see what Chris was talking about.

"Blue Buick. Newer model. Virginia plates. It's been on us since I pulled onto the main road by your house. I didn't think much about it, until now. It's parked across the street."

"Paparazzi maybe?"

"Hoping you're meeting Sierra here at the gun range?" Chris asked, his hand on the door handle as he laughed.

"Maybe. Who the hell knows. These guys are money hungry—" Rick didn't get to finish.

It felt like a hard punch to his chest delivered by an invisible fist. At the same time that Rick was reeling from the percussion, Chris reacted. He leaped forward, yelling something Rick couldn't hear past the rushing in his ear.

The next thing he knew, he was on the ground, Chris on top of him shouting. He didn't understand why.

The only thing Rick could think was to wonder why his hand was wet and warm when he pressed it to his chest just over his heart.

CHAPTER TWENTY-TWO

"So how was it being sequestered with Mr. Hot and Hunky?" Sitting on the bed, Roger waggled his eyebrows as he watched Sierra unpack.

"Please." She rolled her eyes, employing all of her vast acting skills to pretend nothing had happened.

Sure, Sierra felt guilty keeping things from the man who was her best friend. Possibly her only friend. But what was she supposed to do? Admit she'd jumped her bodyguard the moment they'd gotten to the rental house?

"Hmm. I find that interesting."

"What interesting?" Sierra folded Darci's yoga pants and put them on top of the dresser.

"That nothing happened."

"And why is that?" She put Darci's zip-up

sweatshirt and baseball hat on top of the pants. She should have returned everything to Rick before he'd left. She could always get them cleaned and have them delivered to Rick's house. Roger probably had the address.

"Because of the hickey on your neck."

"What?" Sierra touched her throat and leaned toward the mirror. Sure enough, there was a mouth shaped bruise. Clear as day even in the dim light of the bedroom. "Crap."

"Would you like to change your story about nothing happening?" Roger asked. She saw his amused expression in the reflection in the mirror.

"Okay. Fine. It didn't mean anything." She wouldn't have hated it if the relationship had stretched out a bit longer.

At least for as long as she was in town filming, but it was obvious by Rick's demeanor as they packed up to go, and while in the car, that their association ended with the security job.

Roger's eyes widened. "Oh, my, God. Tell me everything."

"Jeez. You're like a teenage girl. There's nothing to tell."

"Is he as hard all over as he looks?" Roger was obviously not letting up. His question had a laugh bursting out of her.

Rolling her eyes at herself and Roger, Sierra couldn't believe she was answering that question, even as she said, "Yeah. He was."

"Girlfriend, I am so jealous I can't even tell you."

"Maybe we should hire security full time."

"Just say the word and I'm on it. Of course, I'll have to interview them all personally. You know, for suitability." Roger smiled before he groaned and stood, digging one hand into his front pocket. "What now? Not that I'm hating the vibrating in my pants after that discussion, but who the hell is calling and bothering me when I'm talking hot men with my best girl?"

Sierra shrugged. "It could be the studio confirming I'll actually be in tomorrow."

"I don't recognize the number." Roger hit the cell to answer and pressed the phone to his ear. "Hello."

She turned back to the open drawer, about to put in her pajamas, when she heard Roger gasp. When she turned back, he was no longer standing. He was sitting on the bed and pale.

He raised his gaze to hers but was still on the phone with whoever the mysterious caller was. "Yes, I understand. Um, can you tell me which hospital he's been brought to?"

Hospital? That connected with the word *him* had Sierra stopping what she was doing to turn her full attention to Roger.

He disconnected the call and focused on her. "Sierra."

"Who is it?"

"Rick."

She reached for the dresser as she felt a little unsteady. "What happened?"

"He was shot."

"Who was that on the phone? His boss Jon?"

"No, the police.

"Was he on anther job?" Did GAPS shuffle their personnel from one assignment to the next with barely an hour downtime in between?

"I don't know. I don't think so. But apparently, it was your stalker."

"They arrested him. Did they let him out of jail?"

"No. They had the wrong guy."

This whole time, he was still out there. And now he'd shot Rick.

Every time he'd taken precautions, she'd mocked him for being too worried.

And now this . . .

Shaking her head, she looked to Roger, at a loss on how to make this all better.

There was no way. All she could do was stand by, helpless, while Rick was possibly dying in the hospital.

Sierra had to sit down herself. It was a lot to wrap her head around. She moved to the bed and collapsed onto the mattress next to Roger.

"It's okay. The police said the guy who shot Rick is dead. You're safe now." He wrapped his arm around her.

Didn't he know she wasn't worried about her own safety? "What happened?"

"I don't have all the details, I'm sure. Here's what I do know. They had a good description of the car. There was police chase, a shoot out, and the cops got him."

"And Rick? How bad . . ." She couldn't finish the question.

"He's in the hospital with a gunshot wound to the chest, but he's alive." Roger ran his hand up and down her back. "But there's more."

"More?" How could there be any more? This was too much already.

"The police located the shooter's hotel room from the information on the rental car he fled in from the scene."

This was important yet all Sierra could think was when did Roger start talking in bad cop show dialogue?

"Sierra, his room was full of pictures. Of you."

"Me?"

"Yeah. From the camera GAPS found in your bathroom."

She'd thought the idea of the camera in her bathroom had been bad before. Knowing a now-dead madman had the pictures in his room made it all worse.

And he hadn't been just spying on her. He'd been trying to kill her. But what didn't make sense is she wasn't even with Rick at the time.

"If he was after me, why did he shoot Rick?"

"The cop on the phone said maybe because he saw Rick as a threat. They don't know for sure."

It didn't matter why. Rick had been shot because of her. She stood. "I want to go to the hospital."

"Sierra, you don't look so great. Maybe you should—"

"Roger, either you take me or I'm calling a cab and going alone."

Finally, Roger nodded. "Okay."

"Thank you."

"I'll call down and have the valet bring my car around." While Roger walked into the living room to make the call, Sierra spun to look at her half unpacked suitcase, before glancing down at the sundress she'd put on.

It could be a long night because she was staying until she was sure Rick was out of danger, no matter how long that took, she didn't care what anybody said.

Should she change clothes? Put on something more comfortable in case she was at the hospital all night?

She realized that if Rick died, she would remember this dress forever as what she'd been wearing when she heard Rick had been shot. It was ruined for her now by the association. She might as well leave it on for the duration of this hell.

Roger appeared in the doorway. "You ready?"

"Yeah." Sierra grabbed her purse and headed for the door.

Getting to the hospital, even with knowing the shooter was dead, was nerve wracking. Every car that drove too closely behind them, or alongside, Sierra looked at with suspicion.

Finally, the hospital came into view.

Roger parked, cut the engine and turned to face her. He covered her hand with his and squeezed before he reached for the door handle to get out. That silent support nearly brought her to tears. They walked together through the doors of the emergency room.

The sounds and smells of the hospital surrounded her, making her queasy. Making it seem all too real. She was shaking by the time they got to the desk to ask about Rick.

"Sierra." The soft female voice behind her had her turning to find Darci. Rick's sister drew her into a hug. "Thanks for coming."

When she pulled away, Sierra could see Darci's red-rimmed eyes. She swallowed hard before asking the question she was afraid to hear the answer to. "How is he?"

"He lost a lot of blood, but the bullet passed straight through and the wound was clean."

"And that's good?" It sounded horrifying to Sierra.

Darci nodded. "Yeah, it could have been a lot worse."

Sierra wasn't sure what to do. Ask to see him? Go find someplace to sit and wait?

Darci hooked a thumb behind her. "You want to come in and sit with me?"

"Can I? Is that allowed?"

"Sure." Darci nodded.

Roger hooked a thumb toward the hallway. "I'm going to find the cafeteria and see how bad the coffee looks. Can I get you ladies something?"

Sierra shook her head. The way she felt, anything she drank might come back up. "No thanks."

Darci held up the can of soda in her hand. "I'm good. Thank you."

"All right. I'll be back." Roger left them.

Darci moved toward a row of curtained partitions, glancing at Sierra as they walked. "He might be sleeping. The painkillers keep him pretty groggy."

"You sure it's okay I'm here?" Sierra felt so out

of place. Darci was Rick's sister. She could sit bedside vigil, but Sierra wasn't a relative.

And when Rick woke up, what would he think seeing Sierra there? She was a client. She was a fling. She wasn't a friend . . . but she could be.

Hell, she wanted to be. A friend. And more.

Why the hell hadn't she realized that before this? She'd been so focused on getting back to work, and on regaining her freedom from stalkers and guards, she hadn't thought about how things had changed between her and Rick. How his absence would leave a hole in her life, even if they had only been together for a short time.

Darci touched her arm. "Sure, it's okay. The guys have been in and out all day. Brody and Chris are still here. I'm just warning you not to expect too much from Rick. He's asleep one minute and then awake and bitching that he wants out of the hospital the next."

That sounded about right. On the verge of tears, overwhelmed with guilt and worry, Sierra still had to laugh.

He was alive and felt good enough to complain. That was such good news, he could bitch all he wanted to and she wouldn't say a word about it.

CHAPTER TWENTY-THREE

"I don't know, bro. You're seeing a helluva lotta action for an old retired guy." Brody's comment to Chris had Rick letting out a short laugh, which he regretted immediately as pain shot through him.

Chris rolled his eyes. "Two shoot-outs in a month is not a lot."

"Hell, yeah it is. I daresay, with the guys you took out on the yacht in Florida last month, you might have more kills under your belt while retired than you did when you were active duty." Brody grinned, obviously enjoying teasing his older brother.

Chris scowled. "Eh, shut up. You know that's not true. And I would have had that guy today if he wasn't out of range."

Brody tipped his head in concession to the point.

"True. I guess you better start carrying your sniper rifle around town, not just your Kimber and Glock. Never know when there's gonna be a shooter speeding away in a car while you're on foot."

"Fuck. If I'd been in the truck instead of on the sidewalk trying to stop Rick from bleeding out I'd have gotten him, even if I'd had to run him off the road to do it."

"It's okay. The cops got him." Rick had to thank God for that, otherwise Sierra would still be in danger.

Brody let out a snort. "They damn well better have. It was the cops who arrested the wrong guy in the first place."

"Now, we can't blame our locals. Those were the assholes in Florida who did that," Chris reminded them.

"Hey, guys. We have a visitor." Darci walking around the partition's curtain had Rick looking her way.

He'd expected one of the guys. Thom and Grant had promised to come back this evening. Who he didn't expect to see was Sierra.

In spite of his shock, Rick managed to say, "Hey."

"Hi. You're awake. How do you feel?"

"Fine. That's why I don't know why they won't let me go home." He raised his voice in hopes a doctor with some authority would hear.

Of course, talking louder hurt like hell but it was worth it. He wasn't pushing that morphine button again. It would only knock him out and he wanted to be awake. Especially now that Sierra was here.

"Rick, you were shot in the chest. I think you need to stay here as long as the doctors say you should." Sierra stepped closer to the bed, making him hate even more than usual the hospital gown they forced him to wear.

He wasn't a damn invalid. He could put on clothes. Okay, maybe not a shirt with all the tubes and stuff, but come on, give a guy a pair of sweatpants or PT shorts, at least.

Rick dismissed her concern. "I'm fine to go home."

"I happen to agree with Sierra, Rick." Darci, the biggest cheerleader for keeping him in the hospital, jumped in to defend Sierra's opinion.

"It's nothing. Tell her, guys. Back me up here." He appealed to Brody and Chris.

Chris laughed. "He has had worse."

"Worse than a shot in the chest?" Sierra's eyes widened.

"Oh yeah." Brody chuckled.

"Great. I really want to hear that." Darci's sarcasm was clear as she huffed and sent the two brothers a look to tell them how unhappy she was.

Rick had tried to keep her in the dark as much as possible when he was active duty. That plan was going out the window pretty fast now.

Chris nudged Brody with his elbow. "Hey, remember when he got that shrapnel in the ass?"

Brody blew out a breath. "How can I forget? I never thought he'd stop whining about it."

Rick frowned. "I didn't whine. And that shit

hurt." He glanced up and realized Sierra was watching the conversation with a completely baffled expression on her pretty face. "Uh, maybe we should change the subject."

She shook her head. "Who are you GAPS guys? Because it's obvious you're not just run of the mill bodyguards."

Brody held up his hands palms forward. "Don't look at me. I'm not part of GAPS. And it's time I get back to base. Text me when you get sprung. I'll see y'all later."

"I might not be home tonight," Chris said as his brother reached for the curtain.

"What else is new?" Brody glanced back and nodded. "Darci. Miss Cox."

Sierra crossed her arms and leveled a gaze on Rick, giving him the impression she wasn't going to be happy until he told her the complete truth.

Chris must have gotten the same impression. He cleared his throat and moved toward Darci. "Come on, darlin'. Let's go grab something to drink."

"I have a—" Darci's eyes widened. "Oh. Okay. Yeah. See you guys in a while."

That rushed exit so he'd be alone with Sierra was not too subtle, but at least he had some privacy. Or as much privacy as a room with walls made of curtains could have.

He swallowed and wracked his brain for small talk when all he wanted to do was grab Sierra and kiss her. "Thanks for coming. I didn't expect a visit."

"You got shot for me. Of course I'd come see

you."

"Well, thank you. I appreciate it."

Her eyes looked a little glassy as she reached out, looking like she was about to take hold of his hand, before she pulled it back and crossed her arms. "Are you really okay?"

"Yeah. I'm fine. I mean, I won't lie to you. It hurts like hell, but the bullet passed right through and didn't hit any vital organs so it's all good." He lifted his one shoulder that wasn't bandaged and in pain.

"How can you be so cavalier?"

"Because like the guys said, I've been shot before, and a lot worse than this."

"How? Where? Why?"

That was a lot of questions for three short words. "Before GAPS, I was with the SEALs. We all were."

Her eyes widened. "Why didn't you tell me that?"

"Because it's not something we go around telling people."

"I'm just *people*?"

He saw the hurt in her eyes. "No. You're not. You know you're not. Look, it was obvious from the night I met you that you assumed I was some dumb mall cop wanna be, so I let you."

"I'm sorry."

"Don't apologize. I could have told you right away. I didn't. I thought it was better to prove to you I knew what I was doing. It doesn't matter. You're safe now. The real guy who was after you is dead and all evidence indicates he was working alone. They will have to let that other guy they're holding go so you might still be getting love notes from him. Be careful, but my instinct tells me he's most likely harmless."

After today, Rick had learned to trust his instincts. If he had done so sooner, he would have paid more attention to the car that trailed them to the range. Hell, he would have never left Ocracoke with Sierra this morning.

"So the good news is, you can go back to your life safely now. And you'll never have to see my ugly face again." He made the joke that hid so much truth and pain.

She moved closer until the skirt of her dress touched the edge of the thin hospital mattress. God how he hated he was in bed for this conversation.

He forced his gaze up and found her biting her lip. "Sierra, it's okay. It's over now. I know it's scary. Everything that's happened—it's going to stick with you for a long while. But it really is over."

Her eyes filled with tears until one spilled over onto her cheek. Rick reached out and grabbed her hand. He'd been here before. Her crying. Him wiping her tear away. He remembered what had happened then. Not much chance of that happening now though. If only there was . . .

Sierra squeezed his hand. "Your face isn't ugly."

She'd picked up on the one silly thing he'd said. To cheer her up, he played up on the joke some more. "No? Maybe I can be in one of your movies."

"I'd like that."

Whoa. Was this Sierra's way of trying to tell him something? Was the ridiculous pipedream of him and her together not so crazy after all?

"Sierra, I know it was a job, but I wanted to tell you that I enjoyed spending time with you. A lot."

For the first time, she looked uncertain. Almost shy. Gone was the overwhelming public persona. "Maybe we should hang out again. That shack you rented wasn't that bad."

Wow. His heart picked up speed. "No, it wasn't. And I'd love to hang out."

"Oh, and by the way, my real name is Carey. Carey Jones. I thought maybe you might want to know that. You know, if we're going to be hanging out together from now on." She lifted one shoulder in a half shrug like it was no big deal.

It felt like a huge step, her confessing her real name to him. Like he'd been given the key to her real life, not just the public one.

"Carey." Smiling, Rick repeated her name, liking how it felt on his tongue to say it. He pulled on her arm, drawing her closer. Wanting more of her to touch him. "Sit next to me."

"I don't want to hurt you."

"You're right. I really am in a lot of pain, but I think a kiss might make me feel much better. And you know, Miss Jones, I did get shot on account of you . . ." His lips twitched with a smile.

"You're a brat." She shook her head at him.

His gaze dropped to her lips as he remembered the feel of them. "I know. So are you."

"I know." She leaned lower and then those lips were pressed against his. He moaned at the feel of what he'd thought he'd never feel again. She pulled back, wide eyed. "Did I hurt you?"

"No. I never felt better." He pulled her down to him again. "Kiss me some more."

"What if your sister and Chris come back in?"

Rick blew out a breath. "They'll deal with it, just like I've had to since they started dating."

She lifted one perfectly shaped brow. "Are we dating?"

Maybe it was the painkillers making him delirious but Rick nodded. "Yup. You okay with that?"

She smiled. "Yes."

"Good." Rick palmed the back of her head and brought her mouth to his, not hating his hospital bed quite as much now that she was in it with him.

If you enjoyed Protected by a SEAL, *please leave a review. And look for the rest of the Hot SEALs series in eBook, print & audio.*

Sign up at catjohnson.net/news to receive notice of new releases.

Hot SEALs

For more titles by Cat visit CatJohnson.net

ABOUT THE AUTHOR

Cat Johnson is a top 10 *New York Times* bestseller and the author of the *USA Today* bestselling Hot SEALs series. She writes contemporary romance featuring sexy alpha heroes and is known for her unique marketing. She has sponsored pro bull riders, owns a collection of camouflage and western wear for book signings, and has promoted romance novels with bologna.

For more titles by Cat visit **CatJohnson.net**
Join the mailing list at **catjohnson.net/news**

44385424R00112

Made in the USA
Middletown, DE
05 June 2017